TRIGOR

BY TOM MERRITT

Copyright © 2019 Tom Merritt

Published by Inkshares, Inc., Oakland, California
www.inkshares.com

Edited by Adam Gomolin and Kaitlin Severini
Cover design by Tim Barber
Interior design by Kevin G. Summers

ISBN: 9781947848894
e-ISBN: 9781950301003
LCCN: 2019931186

First edition

Printed in the United States of America

ACKNOWLEDGMENTS

This story started over lunch with Adam Gomolin from Inkshares, as we brainstormed what Pilot X might do after he destroyed the universe he knew in order to save it for most. Thanks to Adam for the brainstorming that continued well beyond that lunch, into edits and story structure and cover art and more. I also couldn't imagine how this book would have gotten done without the expert guidance of Avalon Radys, who keeps us all on track and makes sure book ideas become books people can actually buy and read. Special thanks to James Thatcher, who provided some logistics insight that made the Matriarch of Trade not only a better character, but hopefully a slight bit more entertaining for people involved in the actual trade industry. Thanks to Kaitlin Severini, whose excellent copy editing polished the work to a shine! Any mistakes you find are mine, not hers. Thanks also to our beta readers who provided essential insights to make the story shine. And an inexhaustible fountain of thanks to all the people who backed the book on Inkshares, giving me the confidence that maybe people were interested in what else old Pilot X was up to. Y'all rock.

BEGINNING

THE OLD MAN led her down the empty hallway in the empty wing. The walls were the gray of an old club. The carpet was deep red and seemed to suck up all the light. She could barely see the dark wooden doors that lined each side of the hall.

"This one," he said, pointing at one of the wooden doors near the end of the hall. "Your things are in there. No one will bother you."

"Thank you," she said.

"All for the Order," the man said, and left her to it.

Inside the room were several stacks of unopened crates and boxes that contained the parts she had worked so hard to get. They had the shipping and customs stamps of multiple worlds on them, as she had routed them through complex trade routes in order to make them difficult to trace. She was probably overdoing it. She didn't need to hide this work so much as keep it a surprise, but she had always been the kind of person to throw herself into things. And besides, what good was the Order's standing offer of help if she couldn't use it for a private project?

She began opening the packages. Each one contained a different piece of what she hoped would eventually become a working, innovative whole. As the packing materials piled up on the floor, the workbenches became populated by dozens of metal boxes in different shapes and with different dials and switches alongside bundles of cables, tubes, and other small parts like gauges. It would have been a jumble of incomprehensible nonsense to most people, but to her it looked like notes in a song, just waiting to be arranged into a melody.

She was the conductor. She smiled at that idea. She was going to compose a song to save the world. She'd no longer be ignored and unappreciated.

She tried to hum a tune and laughed a bit as she began to assemble things and power up components for testing. She laughed a lot when she saw just how well this was going to work. The parts came together just as she had imagined. The flow felt wonderful. She marveled, as what had once been an insane plan turned into a reality under her fingers. She felt the thrill of her intelligence matching with her skill at execution. All of her talents served an unassailable purpose.

And nobody in the universe could stop her.

AWAKE

HE SOBBED.

He had done it.

A hand touched his shoulder. He turned. It was Alexandra.

His sobbing mixed with laughter. "What are you doing here?"

"I hid on the *Verity*," she said, tears falling. "I couldn't let you do it alone."

"Oh, thank you, thank you!" He reached to embrace her, but she stepped back. "What's wrong?" he asked.

"Nothing, I—" She fell backward. Pilot X rushed to grab her, but he was too late. She tumbled down into a deep crater and out of sight.

"There was a seventeen-percent chance she would not survive the Instant," he heard Verity say. "But I didn't calculate her slipping and falling like that."

Pilot X was enraged by Verity's lack of respect. "What have you done!" he shouted, realizing what he said was illogical.

"It's not what I have done at all," Verity said. "And I dislike the implication." She launched the ship into the sky, then disappeared in a flash, leaving Pilot X alone in the wake of destroying the universe.

"No! Verity, come back," he cried. "We have to fix this!"

"It's time for breakfast," she said.

But she wasn't there. Also, he wasn't there. And Alexandra wasn't there. He woke to darkness.

"It's time for breakfast," Verity repeated.

That's right. He was alone. Inside a hut he had built for himself. Not nearly as nice as the one he had once built for someone else, but it kept the sun out. Kept it out very effectively, as it turned out.

"It's time for—"

"Yes, I heard you!" he shouted, and got out of bed.

Outside was a sparse wood, unspoiled by sentient occupation, with two exceptions. One was the poorly made hut that looked like a sad man's faded yellow winter hat dumped in a pile of leaves. The other was the *Verity*. The bright silver-gray cylinder, with its curved glass cockpit window, was three times Pilot X's height but still seemed small somehow. Perhaps because Pilot X knew the timeship hid a singularity compartment that was as big as a planet.

In a clearing between the hut and the *Verity*, Pilot X had set up a pot over a crude and now cold fire pit with a stump for a seat next to it. He sat down on the stump, then took out a plastic jug full of water and used a wooden ladle to add water to the pot. He took salt out of a pocket of his filthy suit and sprinkled some in the water.

He sighed and looked around, scratching his lengthy, dark brown beard. Somewhere under it was a face that itched. His face—in fact, his whole lanky person—would have passed as unremarkable on almost any planet with humanoids. Alendans often tried to fool themselves that they were the prototype humanoid, though there had never been any evidence for that. He had wondered whether, now that the rest of the Alendans were gone, it would be easier to go back in time and discover just how so many humanoid races had evolved. Was it colonization, convergent evolution, or some combination? In fact, there were so many humanoid peoples in the universe, he sometimes wondered if the disappearance of the two major non-humanoid species, the Sensaurians and Progons, had left any other kinds. That kind of thinking would drive him back into his hut, so he stopped it and focused on breakfast.

He searched around near the fire pit for a mound of kernels of the local oat-like plant he planned to boil for breakfast. He found the pile and gathered it up.

"You don't have to do that," said Verity. "I've made you bacon and eggs." The smell of a delicious breakfast drifted out of the ship toward Pilot X.

Humph. He grunted. Verity was an AI who, among her many talents, could reform organic edible matter into different forms that looked and tasted like almost anything you could want. In this case, she had taken legumes and plant matter and converted them into some of the proteins, fat, and other delicious elements of breakfast foods. She had been trying to use those talents to shake Pilot X out of his depression and self-imposed hard living.

"And coffee," she added.

Pilot X dropped the kernels he had collected.

"That's not fair."

A smell like coffee drifted toward Pilot X.

"That's not real," he said.

Verity said nothing.

Coffee was gone as far as Pilot X knew. Coffee had disappeared. Pie had disappeared too. Everyone he knew and loved had disappeared. Three entire species of beings, guilty, innocent, and otherwise, had been erased by Pilot X. He desperately missed coffee almost as much as he desperately missed Alexandra, and the idea that one of the things he loved had returned gave him the nauseous feeling of longing and guilt that he was trying very hard not to feel these days.

"Verity! You can't lie. Is that really coffee somehow?"

"I am unable to synthesize proper coffee, but I have created—"

"Scratch and sniff," Pilot X grunted, and started picking up the kernels he'd dropped.

"Scratch and sniff?" Verity asked, pretending she could not figure out what he meant.

"Yeah. Smells like coffee but isn't."

"It's hot. And brown," Verity suggested in what might have been meant to sound hopeful and pleading.

Pilot X said nothing. He dumped the oat-like bits into the kettle and settled down to make a fire out of leaves and twigs. He did this every morning, struggling for fifteen to twenty minutes before he got the fire to light. Verity did not tell him she remotely started the fire every morning for him.

ALERT

PILOT X SLEPT and dreamed of coffee. He had eaten what he called breakfast, then tired himself out carrying one of the empty plastic jugs to the stream for water. He'd thought about bathing but shrugged it off. It didn't feel properly penitent.

Pilot X was the last Alendan and it was his fault the rest were gone. His people had engaged in a time war with two other species that threatened to tear apart the fabric of space and time. The Alendans outdid them all by making a weapon that could have destroyed all creation. Pilot X stole the weapon and used it to erase the three civilizations from time and reset the universe to a more peaceful version where the time war had never happened.

Pilot X still existed because the user of the weapon, called the Instant, was protected from its effects. But no other Alendans survived. Not the Secretary, who had prosecuted the war. Not Guardian Lau, who had tried to keep the Instant a secret. And not Alexandra. He had barely gotten to know and fall in love with her before he had to erase her from existence. And he felt pretty damn guilty about it. And he felt guilty about feeling guilty about destroying one person, when he had destroyed so many others. Not destroyed. Prevented from existing. Most of all, he felt guilty that he knew that if he were sent back to that exact point with that same choice in those same conditions, he'd do it again.

After fleeing to the farthest edge of the universe, where the people of the Fringe Cascade had heard his story and let him go, he had exhausted his tears and come here. He was hiding, but there was no one looking for him. He could take Verity anywhere in space and time, but instead he stayed here, on an unoccupied planet. He spent his days listening to Verity's pleas, eating boiled kernels and fetching water in a plastic jug, plastic being one of the few luxuries he allowed himself. That, and naps.

"Alert."

Pilot X woke with a start.

"Alert," Verity said again.

Great. Verity had a new tactic. "Oh, just stop." Pilot X shook his head.

"Alert," Verity repeated.

He laughed. It sounded like the auto alert she used to give when he was flying missions. It was not part of her AI system but an autonomic response to any danger that showed up in a scan.

"Alert."

It was very clever of her to imitate it. The autonomic responses to her were like a knee-jerk would be for him. Something he couldn't resist doing if provoked by a hammer on the knee, but something he could fake if he needed to.

"Alert."

"Give it a rest!"

"I'm sorry. It's my autonomous system. You'll need to acknowledge it, or I can't stop it," Verity said in her normal voice.

"Fine, alert acknowledged," he mumbled.

"Scans have detected a time tremor. The tremor matches a signature listed as high danger."

Pilot X squinted. "A time tremor? I thought you said there aren't any more time-traveling species."

"Yes," Verity said. "There are no species dedicated to time travel like the Alendans were. There are some civilizations with minimal chronological technologies."

"A time tremor would need more than minimal," Pilot X scoffed.

"That is true. Would you like me to interpret the findings?"

"You'd like that, wouldn't you? Get me talking. Get me *engaged*. Forget it, Verity. I'm not biting."

"I did not ask you to bite."

"Ha. Humor still coming along, I see."

"I was not attempting humor; I was attempting to interpret the alert for you."

Pilot X just stared at the ship.

"That was an attempt at humor," Verity said.

"Maybe you're not getting as good as I thought. OK. Fine. Interpret it."

"A time tremor was generated, likely as part of a test of a time dilation and space-time-fabric-affecting device. It did not appear to be a transportation device. Its waveform suggests it is meant to reform nodes."

Pilot X almost fell off his stool. "There's only one thing that could ever reform nodes. That's really not funny, Verity."

"I did not say it could reform nodes. I said its waveform suggested it was meant to reform nodes. It did not appear to succeed."

"What does it mean?" Pilot X found himself asking despite his attempt at callousness.

"It certainly is an attempt at chroneon observation. It is also likely to be an attempt of non-transportive timeline adaptation. Examples could include broad effects like climate adjustments or orbital velocities. The level indicates at present that it would only be capable of small effects on very large objects or regions, though it does not appear to be a sustainable beam, hence the lack of any appreciable effect. It is more difficult to determine intention."

Verity had been getting better at translating her precise probability percentages into natural language approximations such as "likely" and "certain." Pilot X was impressed.

"Not a single number in there. Well done, Verity."

"Thank you. Would you like to hear my projections on intentional possibilities?"

Pilot X was softened up. "Sure," he said.

"Someone is trying to create the Instant."

"Oh, sod off," Pilot X snapped.

Verity said nothing.

"How can you know that!? You're just saying that to get a rise out of me. Well, it worked. But not the way you wanted. I'm going into that stinking hut and I'm not coming out."

"I may be wrong," Verity said.

That stopped him. This wasn't some ham-handed psychological trick, or she wouldn't have admitted that. Unless she was so good at psychology now that she could mimic the one actual thing that would make him take notice in a way that was utterly indistinguishable from the real thing. And if she could do that, she would know that he would not be able to risk letting someone create the same device that he had used to destroy his own people. Because that device could also destroy everything. And if there was even a sliver of a chance that it could happen again, he would have to try to stop it. In fact, he might be the only one who *could* stop it.

She would know that. She would know he couldn't resist. So she could, potentially, act in every way like it was true. And in the end, it didn't matter. If she had faked it, he would deal with that later. It would end his relationship with Verity in a way that hiding in his hut could not. She would know that, too. And she wouldn't risk that.

"You're serious," he said.

"I cannot lie."

"I'm beginning to wonder about that. Which makes for a puzzle when you say it, but—you mean it about the time tremor, don't you?

"I do," she said.

"Let me clean up."

RESTORED

HE FOUND HIMSELF in the singing saltwater shower on board the *Verity* before he realized it. He hadn't used it in ages. The salt water scrubbed you down, then the fresh water cleaned the salt out of your hair and off your skin. He always left feeling twice as clean as any other shower. And this particular saltwater shower also sang you a song perfectly tuned to the rhythm of the water.

The music felt moody as he got under the water. He fought off feelings of betrayal as he cleaned. He had promised himself he would not get involved in this universe. He would not expose himself to any responsibility for it. He had saved it. He had been judged. He had been set free. His punishment was to live in this hut. Taking this shower felt like cheating.

But if Verity was right, and someone was re-creating the Instant, well then, that must be an exception to his self-imposed life sentence. He scrubbed under his arms and noticed the music getting intense. After all, there was no one in this universe more experienced with the Instant than he. Wait, that was verging on self-important. Mass murderers like himself didn't get to feel self-important. He had to feel humble.

But did he? He let the water play over his face, taking off weeks of grime. He hadn't murdered people; he had made an irrevocable and unavoidable choice to save the universe. He was its—no. He wasn't going to let himself excuse what he'd done with any kind of messianic notions. The music shifted to a minor key. He may have saved the universe, but he had still eliminated millions and broken himself.

But he hadn't broken the universe. The salt scrub was feeling really good on his calves. The music was pounding out a driving tune now. In fact, the universe, if Verity was right, was about to break itself. And he could fix it.

He stopped scrubbing and the freshwater rinse kicked in.

He could fix this.

For the first time in billions of light-years. He smiled.

READY

HE HATED TO admit it, and wouldn't if pressed, but it felt good to be back in his pilot's chair, looking out the curved window at the stars, knowing that the cramped, efficient ship carried a planet-sized space around in its singularity.

He wondered sometimes what all was in there beyond the singing shower. He hadn't been the first to pilot her. All kinds of things could be hidden away. So much, in fact, that he couldn't possibly find it all. Verity herself could only scan for dangerous items and unknown life signatures, neither of which were ever present. But old notebooks? A classic car from Alenda's motor age? Pie?

Probably not pie. It wouldn't last long outside of a vac-pac and he had never run across any evidence of unidentified vac-pacs. One of the downsides of his planet-sized singularity was that there was likely no secret hidden pie. None edible, in any case. None that wasn't a moldy spot. And he missed pie. He hoped the universe had reinvented pie when it reinvented itself after he activated the Instant. How could it not? Pie was universal, wasn't it? He supposed he could put that to the test. He would make it the secondary mission: to find pie.

Wait, tertiary mission. Obviously, the primary mission was to find out about this time tremor, or he never would have left his hut. And his tertiary mission would certainly be to find pie. But almost more important than the potential destruction of the universe, and solidly the secondary mission, was to find coffee. If he was going to be bothered to venture out into this potentially broken universe, where he would be reminded by every speck of dust that he had committed specicide three times over, then he was damn well going to get some coffee out of it.

It had been the first thing he ran out of. He hadn't had any pie on board when he destroyed the universe. Bad planning, that. But he had stowed away some coffee. Not nearly enough. He had rationed it to one glorious cup every sleep cycle, but it eventually ran out. And the planet where it had been discovered was obscure now. All he had to go on were oblique references in a few texts from his universe to a planet that may or may not still be the birthplace of coffee. It was a dual planet: one water, one arid. Coffee had come from the water one. It was around a middle-aged star. It had ice caps. It smelled like rain. Or at least that's what one poetic travelogue said. But where? That, the records did not explain.

"Verity, are you running the water-planet scanner?"

"Our mission is to investigate the time tremor," she said.

"Sure, but we can have other missions too. You're capable of doing what, one million things simultaneously?"

"No, but it's a lot. And some of them are keeping the cabin pressurized and full of oxygen and things like that. If I drop one in order to look for coffee, you might die. Would you like me to look for coffee?"

Damn. Her humor was starting to develop into sarcasm. He had to admit, he liked it.

"I want you to not kill me, all right? But we can scan for water planets as we go, no?"

Verity said nothing.

"I mean, we—"

"I have entered scanning for water planets that fit the known descriptions of the coffee planet in an adjunct slot that can be overridden by any necessary or main mission-critical functions. Is there anything else I can do for you?"

"Thank you, Verity. What can I do for you?"

"Find the time tremor," she said. That was terse for Verity.

"This has you worried, doesn't it?"

"I cannot worry in the same way you can, but it has created a similar pattern of anticipations that may manifest themselves to you as worry."

"You're worried!" Pilot X said. He was too.

PARTHIAN PRIME

VERITY JUMPED TO the most likely of several stellar systems that might be the origin of the time tremor. They arrived at the moment right before the time tremor had happened so they could attempt to detect it again and get a more precise location. As they orbited out among the system's gas giants, waiting, Verity scanned the system's broadcasts to get some background information.

"It seems to be called the Parthian System," said Verity. "There is no analogue from—your—our—the old universe. The most inhabited body is a rock giant called Parthian Prime. It claims to be the origin of the system's civilization, but interestingly, several other planets and moons also claim to be the origin of the system's civilization. Among them are a planet that calls itself Original Parthia, one called Parthian Reál, one just called Parthia, and a moon called Parthian Landing. There are other inhabited moons, but no others that claim to be original. Only Parthian Prime would have had the natural ecosystem to evolve intelligent life, but the other locations claim that the Parthians migrated here from another system and modified their original planets before colonizing Parthian Prime. This seems unlikely but not impossible, especially if there was some collapse in society after a colonial landing. Which happens to be the dogma of the citizens of Parthian Landing.

"Despite the conflict over primacy, the civilization is quite united in a federal system and is the largest trading civilization in history, hence the large number of inhabited planets and moons. We have arrived in the middle of the height of Parthian Civilization."

"How do you know?"

"I jumped us forward while you were napping."

"Stop doing that. It ruins my sleep. Messes with my circadian rhythm or something."

"You wouldn't have noticed if I hadn't told you."

"Still."

"In any case, we have not felt the time tremor yet, so you may go back to sleep and I will not jump again while . . ."

"While what?"

"Update. I have detected the time tremor."

Pilot X sat up straight. "Where to?"

"Odd."

"Where's odd?"

"No, the reading is odd."

"Why is it odd?"

"It's backward."

"What?"

"Backward."

"Yes, but what does that mean?"

"I have detected the time tremor. Its signal does not locate it here, but this location echoes the origin."

"I believe you just made me more confused."

"Imagine the time tremor is point A."

"*Point A* is not a very imaginative name, but OK. I have imagined a beautiful point A filled with flowers and unicorns and a time tremor."

"Now imagine two cones with the narrow ends at point A. Each expands away from point A in a different direction. One forward in time and one backward."

"Two delicious pecan praline ice cream cones are at an angle to the frolicking piles of unicorns that is point A."

"One cone starts with the time tremor and its cone is its effects. The other cone is the prior actions and effects that brought the time tremor into existence."

"One cone is melting and the other freezing?"

"Not far-off," said Verity with what, in someone else, might be described as a hint of admiration. "We are in the cone of actions and effects that brought the time tremor into existence. It came from here. But it isn't here."

"Parts! You're talking about the parts they used to make it," Pilot X said.

"Possibly. If the parts to build the"—she stopped herself from saying the Instant; they both danced around saying it—"device were from here, that could cause this cone-like reading."

"Well, we're here. And time is on our side. Might as well take a look. Any particular original Parthian planet likely to be the source of the parts?"

"It is hard to say. As I mentioned, this is the universe's largest and most successful trading society at its height. But in my estimation, the highest probability of finding information would result from visiting Parthian Prime, which is the location of the central-trade administrations."

"To Parthian Prime then!"

HUNTERS

A DARK TRIANGLE of a ship lurked off the ecliptic of the stellar system, hiding from the Parthian Trade Enforcers. Prellix Scalgote piloted and commanded the ship. She was a freelancer often referred to as an "arm of the Syndicate." That meant she did dirty work for the people who paid her. And she loved dirty work.

Prellix was strong. Tall and muscular with sturdy arms and legs and a shock of pink hair above a scowl that told you to get lost if you knew what was good for you. Growing up in the industrial suburbs of Semblanz V—the most boring planet in existence—all her friends had dreamed of winning the lottery or marrying rich or becoming an important officer. She dreamed of busting heads. Well, she didn't dream; she actually busted a lot of heads on Semblanz V. But she dreamed of busting heads and getting paid for it.

She wanted to command her own ship and she did. Except, she was also the first officer, cook, medic, and chief engineer. That was because her shipmate, Paul, was useless. Dumpy Paul. He was short and weak and everything else that was the opposite of Prellix. And he adored her.

She didn't like to think about Paul. She didn't tend to acknowledge Paul even when he was there. Paul, also from Semblanz V, was a necessary evil. She couldn't avoid him, so she worked around him like she would work around a broken part she couldn't afford to repair. She had her orders. Her orders were to operate this ship with Paul and do what the Syndicate told her. And literally, right now, the Syndicate was telling her to look for something.

"You'll know it when you encounter it because it will be of immense value compared to the usual flotsam and jetsam you drag in," said the disguised voice of the Secret Man, her Syndicate contact. "I want it. You'll know it. You'll steal it. Right?" the man's voice commanded.

"Right," said Prellix, not just because her shadowy boss ordered it. Not just because she had seen what happened to a few others who failed the Syndicate. (It involved their insides usually ending up as their outsides.) But because it also sounded like her kind of fun.

"I am on it, sir," she said. "Gotta go." She had just spotted something that looked insanely valuable.

"Excellent," said the secret voice, and ended the connection.

"Did you see that?" she shouted to Paul.

"See what? That was an audio call," said Paul, as if waking from a nap despite the fact that his eyes had been open for hours.

"No, that ship." She pointed at a reading on her screen. "It's got a drive signature that's unexplainable. I've never seen anything like it. Something quantum but no idea what. And the weight-class sensor is impossible. Nothing that heavy could fly."

"Huh, must be faulty," said Paul, settling back into his eyes-wide-open nap.

"No, idiot. The sensors are fine. That thing is valuable. We need it."

"But it's gone."

Prellix didn't bother to answer. She got on the coms. She had saved up a little leverage over a few important people just for this sort of situation. She was going to get paid. Paul was not.

PERMISSION

"THEY ARE NOT accepting the story," Verity said.

For the first time since he had fled to the Fringe Cascade, Pilot X was trying to land on a civilized planet with decent traffic control. That meant he had to establish who he was and why he was there. This was difficult for him. He flew in a time-ship that shouldn't exist; he was from a race that didn't exist; and he had absolutely no credentials. He shouldn't, in fact, be there.

"Wait. I have an idea," he said. "Tell them we were set upon by pirates."

"I don't think that will work," said Verity.

"Try it."

There was a pause while Verity tried it.

"It worked," she finally said.

"I figured—wait, what?!"

"I told them we were attacked, and our ship was damaged and needs repair."

"Oh. Well, all right then."

"You'll need to show them some kind of damage."

"We'll worry about that later."

Pilot X guided Verity down toward the ice-blue oceans of the planet below. It was mostly shallow water with strands of land strung out in long dotted lines along the surface. Civilization centered on a few of the largest islands. They descended toward a heavily inhabited strip that looked like two question marks joined at the bottom. In the bar that joined the two was the spaceport where Pilot X had been instructed to land.

At first it looked like there wasn't much room for a spaceport, but as they got closer it became apparent that the island was much larger than it looked from orbit. In fact, a vast city full of towering buildings populated the isthmus that connected the two longer strands, which were less dense and quite rocky.

Their flight path took them across the length of the city, giving them an amazing view of the skyline. The towers, which looked mostly white from the air, turned out to be thousands of shades from silver to gray to granite, all reflecting the ice-blue waters that surrounded them. The architectural styles varied from long, pointed needles to boxy functionalism to gravity-defying structures for which Pilot X had no name.

As they descended, the city shone around them.

"They want us to set down for repairs in a pretty nice-looking place," Pilot X said.

"Parthian Prime is considered Parthian Prime's third most beautiful city," Verity reported.

"Third? What are the other—wait, Parthian Prime is the name of the city *and* the planet?"

"Yes, it is the planet's second oldest city."

"Fine, I'll ask. Since you so clearly want me to. What's the oldest city called?"

"The oldest city and the one that is also considered most beautiful is called Parthia."

"Can I just skip to the part where you explain all of this?" He was enjoying the view so much, he was only barely annoyed.

"Their history says Parthia is the oldest city and in ancient times, explorers from there founded Parthian Prime. It surpassed Parthia in its population and prominence and gave rise to the name of the planet. This story conflicts with other accepted histories about why this planet is called Parthian Prime. However, all histories agree that the city and planetary names are linked. The city considered second most beautiful is called Latroy. It is a vacation city spread out over an atoll thousands of meters long. People can swim from one island to the next across the whole city and often spend weeks doing so. Special hotels called Atolleeies—"

"That's fine. Hey, so why do they want us to make the repairs here?"

"Parthian Prime is home to the Trade Ministry, and as such is the official repair and inspection headquarters for trade vessels."

"Makes sense."

"How will we explain that we do not have the damage that we claimed?" Verify asked.

"I'll handle it."

Verity set down in an open landing lot for nonstandard craft. Pilot X stood with his hand resting on the latch to open the cockpit. Suddenly he didn't want to be here. He wanted to be in his hut. No, that wasn't right. What he really wanted was to be on Alenda. He wanted to be in a universe that didn't have the Instant and had never needed the Instant to be used. But he couldn't do that, so he wanted to hide in his hut as punishment. He was about to take his hand off the latch. But if he did that, this universe might create an Instant, he reminded himself. The singing shower song played in his head. This new universe might destroy itself and him with it. Would that be so bad? The hand wavered again. *Yes. It would be,* he told himself sternly. He could not live even a short life knowing he was letting a second universe be destroyed. He could fix this.

He took in a deep breath, pasted a smile on his face, and turned the latch. He left the cockpit and began walking toward the nearest building without waiting for anyone to approach. This would be standard procedure for a normal cleared incoming vessel. You just head to the nearest building, which is almost always processing, whether it's immigration or customs or whatever the local bureaucracy calls for.

It was not standard procedure, if you had just told the landing agency that you were damaged by pirates and couldn't properly send idents and needed repair and probably special attention from some kind of legal agency.

Pilot X wasn't surprised when three Parthian Prime people in uniforms began running toward him and shouting before he could get to the doors of the building. He maintained his pasted-on smile and did his best to look surprised.

"Please return to your craft," was the only thing Pilot X could make any sense of. The rest were shouting over one another. He was slightly disappointed to find that Parthians appeared to be common bipedal humanoids with their mouths in their heads. Their familiar form didn't make them any more intelligible to him.

So he pretended confusion. "Oh? OK. Usually I just go process my ident when I land. Is this new? Oh! Or is there some kind of action going on? I'm so sorry. They didn't say anything when I was landing."

The group stopped short in front of him. The three Parthians varied in height but all wore crisp white uniforms with blue piping. Their slicked-back short hair had varying shades of brown on each head. It reminded Pilot X of wood paneling.

"You're the ship that couldn't identify yourself because of damage, right?" said the leader, whose hair had the most dark brown strands.

"What?"

"Your ship. We landed you here because you had damage. That's what we were told."

This is what Pilot X had hoped to hear. In any sufficiently large bureaucracy, some cooperation from those being processed, in this case Pilot X, was necessary to prevent confusion. Because, while the reason for an action might be known by some originating party, in this case landing control, the orders to take that action were often handed down through several different levels to a group that only knew the barest details about it. This was the weakness Pilot X had expected to be able to exploit. The phrase "That's what we were told" was exactly the kind of thing that indicated this was the case.

Pilot X shrugged. "My ship isn't damaged"—not a lie—"I just landed where they told me to"—also not a lie. Also, using the word *they* shifted the officers into the mind-set of thinking it was someone else's problem, whereas *you* would have put them on the defensive.

"Well, something got lost in the translation then—again."

Ah, the word *again*. Music to Pilot X's ears.

"Look, I'll cooperate with whatever you need me to do. But you don't need to send a repair crew or anything. There's nothing to repair."

"What make is that ship?" the shortest one with lightest brown strands asked. "I don't recognize it."

"TC130 out of Belair by way of Pantoon," he said fast, even though what he said didn't make much sense. Quick responses were less suspicious.

"Pantoon? The silent planet? They don't let anyone land there," the leader of the group said, looking confused. The short one started to look suspicious. The medium-height one who hadn't spoken kept looking back the way they'd come. He had the look of someone who had left a delicious slice of pie only halfway through eating it, in order to deal with something that he wasn't convinced was worth the interruption.

"Oh, I didn't land there. Stupidest circuit route I've ever been assigned, but I fly where they tell me. I can tell you all understand."

That got some nods.

The leader spoke into a communication device. "Stand down repair, Bilson. We've got this."

A burst of static seemed to satisfy the leader that his message was heard.

"Look, we'll just head into processing here with you and get this taken care of. That way we did our job, you get processed, and everybody's able to go on their way. The normal processing is done two lots over, but it will just be easier to do it here."

The short one started to object, but the leader interrupted her and said, "Get a form 1735 underway and we'll scan and ident him, Alena." She closed her mouth, then turned and headed toward the building. "Come along . . . uh?"

The name Alena rang through Pilot X's head.

"I'm sorry, what's your name?" the leader asked.

"Oh. Sorry. Pilot X."

"X, huh? Interesting last name. Belairian?"

"On my mother's side," he lied.

The leader nodded, not wanting to think about it too much.

That bit about running an ident troubled Pilot X. He and Verity had successfully bluffed their way into landing, but if his ident didn't show up—which it wouldn't—they would call it in, and the discrepancy between his two stories would come out.

GRANTED

HE ANSWERED ALL their questions truthfully and then they did an ident scan of his DNA. A regular trader should show up with a full record. A resident of an allied civilization would have at least a name and an image. Someone from elsewhere would just show origin civilization and maybe approximate age, etc.

He was going to show nothing. He was the only Alendan in the universe, and as far as the universe was concerned, Alendans never existed.

He began to try out a few different story lines in his head as he waited for the scan results to come back negative, but instead they showed up as *Pilot [BLANK] X, Cargo and Circuit Small Passenger Pilot. Ship: Verity. Origin: Belairian on mother's side.*

Verity had done something. He knew it. And she'd almost pulled it off, but her attempt at humor with his origin tripped things up.

"Ha. You weren't kidding about your mother. But that's not really an acceptable entry. How about your father?"

"Bentrian," he made up.

Alena, the shortest one, dutifully entered *Bentrian* and a red warning bar appeared.

"Well, this doesn't shock me given the weird way your origin was entered previously, but it tripped a trade warning. It's not as bad as it sounds. It just means Bentrian isn't a race we've traded with, which is pretty rare. Congrats. You're the first. We'll need someone at trade to sign off on it. Just a formality. But it will take a minute. There's a waiting room through that door to the left. It's not much, but there're a few chairs and coffee."

He was starting to drift away, contemplating why someone with a name like Alena could look so little like someone named Alexandra, when what she had just said sunk in. "Coffee?" Pilot X tried to keep himself from shrieking.

"Yeah, it's not all that great, but it's hot and black. I used to never drink the stuff. Didn't even have it where I grew up. But everything from everywhere comes through here, so we take advantage. We even have pineapples. Though who can afford those?" She laughed and the other two, even the bored officer, laughed, so Pilot X laughed too. He thanked them and hurried into the waiting room.

On a shelf, as if on a pedestal for veneration, sat a glass pitcher half-filled with black liquid. The smell transported Pilot X. He was certain, logically, that this was bad coffee. In fact, it was probably old and cold.

But he didn't care. It was coffee. Real, honest coffee. This universe was not a total abomination. He took a cup that was made out of some thin, slick material and poured some coffee in it. It was hot. He smelled that familiar smell. It smelled like home. He took a sip. Its magic, dark taste covered his tongue and it wasn't cold. He couldn't tell if it was bad or not. He felt the flavor fill his mouth like a memory and the warmth slide down his throat like a welcome. He imagined the caffeine working its way into his veins to revive him. He let out a sound of pure satisfaction.

"Oh dear, let me make you some fresh," Alena said, taking the cup out of his hands and pouring it out along with everything in the pot. She busied herself making a new pot and set it to brew. It wasn't any kind of brewing system Pilot X was familiar with. The pot was full of water and the darkness began to infuse itself in from the bottom somehow.

"So where are you from?" she asked casually while he waited for the coffee.

Did she know the effect of this torture? Did she know how awful it was to let him have one sip and then take it away like that? If she did, it was a well-executed page from an interrogation manual.

"All over," he said, giving the tried-and-true answer of a military brat. "My parents were in the trade service. Well, my mother was. My dad died when I was very young."

None of this was actually a lie. Pilot X's dad had died when he was very young. His mother had been in the Alendan trade service, and she died when he was still in flight school. And given that he was, in fact, from a version of the universe that no longer existed, "all over" seemed perfectly accurate to him.

Alena nodded. "Yeah, I know a lot of friends like that. Did you have at least one place you stayed long enough to think of as home?"

This felt like a real question, not just fishing for info. Which meant it was the most expert way of fishing for info. Was she really a low-level officer?

"Belair, I guess," he said, because he had been there once. He should never have lied about his mother being Belairian, but then he couldn't have very well said Alendan.

"You don't look Belairian. Must take after your father. What was he again?"

"Bentrian," Pilot X coughed. An even bigger lie. The made-up planet. "I think the coffee is done," he almost shouted. He got another cup and poured some, greedily taking a sip and burning his tongue and enjoying every moment. When his attention returned, another person had joined them. A tall woman with shoulder-length black hair streaked with gray, wearing an immaculate blue-and-yellow suit. He would have thought it garish, but the yellow parts were just so expertly subtle that it made him feel like he was underdressed. Her deep, dark brown eyes encompassed the whole room and left nothing unobserved. He barely noticed the rest of her, given those eyes.

"Matriarch of Trade?!" Alena said, forgetting her line of inquiry.

"Yes, Alena. I got the message about Mr. X's issues here and was close by, so I decided to inquire personally. I do this from time to time, Mr. X, in order to make sure I still understand how my department works. I'm the Matriarch of Trade."

Pilot X had a momentary impulse to curtsy. He knew he was supposed to do something slightly ritualistic from the look the Matriarch gave him.

"Thank you for your interest in my small troubles," Pilot X managed to say.

The Matriarch laughed. "Delightful. So, it seems you're part Beltrian. Is that right, Mr. X?"

"Please, call me Pilot X. We have no titles but our first names where I'm from, and I'm a pilot," he said, forgetting that was a tradition of the nonexistent Alendans and a fairly dead giveaway if anyone cared to do some research.

"A Beltrian custom. Magnificent. I've never heard of it. But then, I've never heard of the Beltrians. Nobody has. Where is it? Is the planet called Beltria?" He could not escape her eyes. He realized that she was saying his made-up planet's name wrong. It calmed him to avoid what seemed to be a trap.

"I'm Bentrian, not Beltrian. Perhaps that's causing the confusion," he said, and laughed.

The Matriarch joined him and filled the room with a slightly insincere mirth. "Bentrian. Of course. My apologies. It's not on any of our charts. Where is it?" She smiled.

Well, that didn't work. He decided to mix in a little truth to see if it would make the lie slide down the throat easier. When he thought about it that way, it made him worry that they'd gag, but he tried it anyway.

"My planet is in the eastern sector of the quarter elliptic around a middle-range star. I can give you the coordinates." He coughed as he said it, and forced a smile. That was how he would have once described Alenda. In this universe, it described the planet where he had been living. There just wasn't anyone on it but him. And it wasn't called Bentria. It wasn't called anything. That's why he'd picked it. It was unknown.

"Please, I'd love to pinpoint it and update our records. Alena, could you?"

Alena went over to an empty space on the wall and drew a square on it with her finger. Suddenly the space within her imaginary square came alive with menu options and graphics. She tapped a bit and a star field appeared, with spaces to enter standard X, Y, Z coordinates. Alena raised an eyebrow and motioned for him to enter the information for Bentria.

He walked over to the wall and something made him say, "It's also called Alenda sometimes. I don't know if it would be filed under that."

Alena and the Matriarch both laughed. The Matriarch said, "Well, I hope it isn't that obscure. But I admire the joke. *Fairy Tales from the Fringe Cascade* is one of my favorites."

Oh no. Had he become a bedtime story? Well, apparently, the main character was not called Pilot X, or he would have already been mocked. He laughed good-naturedly and put in the coordinates for Alenda, which now signified the planet with his shack, population one, which he had decided just now, was called Bentria. He was king, prince, and populace of the Bentrians now.

"That *is* off the beaten path," Alena mused.

"Quite so," the Matriarch agreed. "Please update our charts with the information and add it to Mr. . . . Oh, I'm sorry, *Pilot X*'s records. I think that's all we'll need from you, Pilot X. But I apologize for the confusion and delay. Perhaps there's something else I can do for you? To make up for it, hmm?"

Alena scowled at this, but she slowly closed the screen and left the room.

After Alena was gone, the Matriarch smiled a warm smile. "You can keep your coffee if you like. But there's more and better in my office and it would be more comfortable for us to talk there. Shall we?" She motioned toward the door.

"That's very kind of you, but I couldn't impose any more than I already have," he said, worried about going somewhere unknown with this deeply suspicious and apparently powerful person. He figured his best bet was get back to Verity and start searching for factories or warehouses that dealt in the kinds of parts that made up the Instant.

"Not at all." She looked sincerely warm this time when she smiled. "You have a good face. And I feel truly bad about the mix-up. I'd love to help you if there's any way we can. Would you do Parthian Prime that favor?"

She wasn't going to give up. He could tell. And—he realized— if anybody knew where the kinds of parts that made up the Instant might have come from, it ought to be Parthian Prime's Matriarch of Trade. He'd just have to figure out how not to get trapped while convincing her to give him the info he needed. Easy. He let out an inward sigh and said, smiling, "How can I refuse?" He was, after all, fairly sure that there was no way he could.

Outside the processing building, three new guards waited for the Matriarch. They opened the doors to an enormous floating silver barge.

"My car," she said, letting him board first. A gleaming metal ramp without a speck of dust lowered itself down. He walked up and found that the top of the barge was covered by unbelievably thin glass, or at least something transparent. He resisted touching it for fear of putting the first fingerprint ever on it. Everything in the car was spotless and shining. The interior was a dark black cloth, very soft to the touch and comfortable to sit on. The controls, dials, and handles were chrome. The three guards—assistants—whoever they were—got in behind him and took up most of a four-seat semicircle. He assumed one of them must be driving. The Matriarch boarded last and sat across from Pilot X.

The couch was so comfortable, he felt like if he hadn't been worried about an inevitable betrayal from the Matriarch, he could lean back and drift immediately off to sleep. But he didn't. He also declined her offer of a drink. But he craved something to make him feel a bit more at home.

He couldn't stop himself from asking, "Do you have pie on Parthian Prime?"

The Matriarch cocked her head. "The number?"

"No, it's a kind of food," he said.

"Oh! I don't think we do. I don't think I've heard of it, anyway."

"A shame. It goes so well with coffee."

"What is it?"

Pilot X thought hard about how to respond. "Delicious," he answered.

The Matriarch laughed again, filling the car to bursting.

They rode in silence after that. The Matriarch stared at a device Pilot X assumed let her communicate with people she needed to communicate with about important things. This must have been a polite time to do such things because she made no attempt to apologize or engage Pilot X in conversation.

He spent the time looking out at the city, which was as clean and shining as the car's interior. He wondered how they did it. Dust-repellent molecules? Nano-cleaners? He began to realize the wonder of not knowing anything about the universe. He had known a lot about the old universe, and he had never heard of Parthian Prime. All trade had been dominated by his race and the two others they'd warred with. If Parthian Prime existed then, it was not a trading power, not even a minor one.

He had everything to discover and a nearly endless universe to discover it in. That realization began to stir the idea that he could have a reason to live beyond his guilt. It made him doubly sure about his decision to stop the Instant from being re-created. He imagined Verity reminding him that it had been her idea, and laughed.

"What is so funny?" the Matriarch asked.

He hadn't realized he was laughing out loud. "I'm sorry, just thinking about a friend. Your city is amazing. So beautiful and clean."

"Thank you. Many trading societies think having effective trade is all docks and dust and the grimier it is the better. Our society thought better of that and many, many years ago a woman named Federiqua Martelxes created a small one-celled organism that eliminated ugliness."

Pilot X scowled. "Eliminated ugliness?"

"Oh, there's some more scientific explanation for it, I'm sure." She waved her hands. "Someone tried to explain it to me once. Something about an appetite for absorbing certain molecules tied to environmental conditions, blah blah blah. I just know it works," she said. "And that we all have a glass of Shand-ade on Federiqua's Day and throw the ritual dust bombs into the street and see for a few minutes what our city would look like without her."

"Sounds fun," Pilot X mused.

"It is. But not as fun as watching new visitors see our city. I get used to how clean and bright and gorgeous it is." She laughed. "Until I see it again through a visitor's eyes."

She leaned over by him and began to point out certain landmarks as they drove. A tower with a huge ball at the top that looked like it was made entirely of glass was the Parthian Government building. A swirling building that had interlocking spirals within which you could see people walking was a trade insurance conglomerate's headquarters.

"And look way down there. Do you see that rather dark building sort of lost between the two metallic skyscrapers?" Her face was startlingly close to his. It had been a long time since he had been close to any other people, and he had to stop himself from screaming, punching her, or kissing her, or all three.

Instead he made a show of squinting and saw what looked like a three- or four-story structure made of some kind of brick, with about a dozen unusual square spires all over its top. "Yeah, that one with the chimneys?"

"Yes, that's it," the Matriarch said. She leaned in closer to him, her voice getting softer as she explained. "That's called Parthian Hall. It's the oldest building on the planet. It was originally a home for a wealthy trader. Not the first in Parthian Prime, but one of the pioneers. Later, Federiqua Martelxes was born there. It's still an occupied house. People still live there!" She leaned back but touched his arm. "Many of our old buildings survived for centuries as founding tradesmen's landmarks, but as nostalgia for these things faded, fewer and fewer were protected. If it weren't for Federiqua being born there, this one probably would not have survived either. It's held by a private family, but they offer tours of the tradesman's office and

Federiqua's bedroom a few days a week. An interesting sight if your business permits." She let go of him with a look that had absolutely no relation to the museum tour she had just suggested.

Then he realized she'd mentioned his business. She was fishing for information and using her best bait. He wondered if it worked on people who had not been isolated from their entire civilization and spent several months living alone in a hut.

Eventually they pulled into a parking garage below a relatively mundane mirrored building in the shape of a parallelogram. The car drove through a dark cement tunnel that was incongruously clean for being vehicle access. It exited onto a smooth, pearl-colored platform with bright lights shining down like the car was on a showroom floor, though the platform was only big enough for one car. A distant hum and the tiniest rumble was the only indication Pilot X had that they were moving. After a surprisingly short period of time they arrived on the roof of the massive building.

"Welcome to the Parthian Prime Trade Center." The Matriarch held her hands up dramatically and beamed as she led Pilot X out of the car and onto the rooftop. It was a clean gray surface, spotted here and there with plants and bordered by short walls covered in ivy. In one corner was a wooden bar with a red-velvet shade over it. A man in some kind of formal black attire stood behind it. She grabbed Pilot X by the hand and led him over to the bar.

She primly let go of the hand with a downcast look as they got to the bar. "This is my office when the weather is good." She pulled up a bamboo-like stool and motioned for Pilot X to sit. "When it rains, they have to pull up the walls and cover the whole roof," she said, waving over at the edges of the roof while sitting down on her own stool. She leaned in toward him just a hair closer than you might expect and asked, "Would you like a drink? Let me guess." She touched his knee briefly. "Coffee?" Pilot X nodded, and the Matriarch asked the man behind the bar for two coffees.

The man went over to something that looked exactly like a Lendrik Perfe-Drip coffee maker. It couldn't be, since the Lendrik company disappeared along with the rest of Alenda, but Pilot X marveled and almost cried to see the signature inverted-steel funnel that led down into glass tubing to deliver the perfect cup of drip coffee.

"Is that—" Pilot X waved toward the machine as the man pulled two cups of coffee from it. "What is that?"

"Oh, that's one of our few homegrown products. The Kadrik Coffee-Drip. Have you had coffee from it before? It's marvelous."

The man in the formal attire set a cup of coffee in front of each of them. Pilot X didn't hesitate to take a sip.

It almost knocked him off his seat. The processing office's coffee had transported him; it had been so long since he had had real coffee. This coffee, made well in a proper device, not only transported him, it white-glove-delivered him with free setup, color balancing, and continuing support.

"It's good," he said. "Such a shame you don't have pie."

"We'll have to look into it." The Matriarch led them over to some comfortable lounge chairs.

"So. What do you think of our city?"

It seemed perfect. Pilot X thought it was right that an endless time war seemed to have been replaced with such an admirable civilization ruling large parts of space-time, even if it did rule by trade. It didn't heal him, but it helped. Like getting a new dog. You still missed your old one, but it helped. Some. A small part of himself let go and enjoyed the view.

"It's beautiful," he said.

"I'm so glad you think so. But enough about us. Tell me about you. Is there anything I can do to help you in your business here?"

Pilot X imagined Verity shouting *no!* He glanced at his watch, which would let him contact Verity and ask her. He didn't. The Matriarch was so accommodating. So warm. The city was so perfect, so beautiful; they had let him go from processing without any questions. They had coffee. He couldn't let all that be destroyed. They could help him fix things. He blurted out what was on his mind.

"I'm tracking some parts that passed through here. They were shipped out to a buyer and I need to find out who it was. I'm the customs broker for it."

The Matriarch nodded. The obvious question would be why he needed to know that.

"I'd love to help you with that," the Matriarch said. Pilot X stifled his sigh of relief. "Why do you need to know, though?" He stifled his groan of regret. His wrist buzzed. He glanced at his watch. It showed one simple word: *Duties*. So. Verity was listening.

"Duties," he said. "See, the parts were fulfilled from here. Possibly even manufactured or assembled here? But my firm handles the customs transaction fulfillment. We're a customs brokerage and third-party logistics provider and as such, liable for customs, duty, and tax tracking and customer support. In this case, we need to confirm that the correct confirmations of authority were sent, for trade-agreement purposes."

It was the kind of babble he threw out to confuse someone into agreeing with him.

"Well, surely you could have off-loaded that contract onto a local service provider with an indemnity?" The Matriarch smiled.

Oh, right. She was the Matriarch of Trade for the biggest trade civilization in history, at its prime.

"We could have." He laughed. "Should have." Then he shook his head. "But—well—my boss has this client on a short list of essentials and in addition to that, our Power of Attorney ties us up pretty well. We certainly could get away with contract-service tracking, but then we wouldn't be able to deliver the fine touch my boss prefers here. Plus, that wouldn't follow the letter of the POA." He was almost certain that made sense.

She raised her eyebrows. "Quite a client." She set her coffee down. "But I know the type. And I know the wasted hours that go into hedging your bets against all manner of potential slights. It probably won't be worth your trouble, but just in case it is—you have to do it, right?" She shrugged and gave him an understanding nod. "Well, I was right about you. You *do* need my help." She laughed. "So. What are these parts?"

Pilot X didn't have a list of parts. He hadn't thought that far ahead. "I don't know the proper names off the top of my head. If you don't mind?" He raised his wrist.

"Of course. What a funny device. Most of us just implant them. But please, go ahead."

He pretended to use it so she wouldn't catch on that Verity was listening. She probably assumed it was some kind of remote-data-accessibility thing. But from the moment he looked down at his wrist, it had shown the phrase *Diotronic Actuator Potentiometer.*

He started to read the name, but the Matriarch interrupted him.

"Oh, goodness no. I'd never remember it, any more than you. Now that you have it, just hold on to it and I'll fetch someone to handle this for us. Wait here. I'll be right back."

Later, Pilot X felt he should have realized that it was odd for the Matriarch to go off on her own to get something rather than calling a guard or an assistant.

Instead he leaned back and relaxed, possibly for the first time in this universe. Not fully, but perceptibly. He looked at the crystal-clear sky hanging behind the gleaming silver-and-blue skyline around him, dotted by spots of greenery. He noticed the bartender standing motionless and decided to get another coffee. He motioned, but the bartender didn't budge. Android?

"Can I get another coffee?" he asked.

At first the bartender did not react. Then, with a slight head twitch, it said, "Of course," and went about mechanically refilling his coffee. Android.

SCHEMING

THE MATRIARCH HUSTLED into her actual office; the line she had told Pilot X about her office being on the roof was a complete lie. The roof did close when it rained, and she could command everyone out, but she'd never conduct her business out in the open like that. What a rube he was to buy that line. Her still spacious but much more efficient quarters had all the secure devices she needed, constant data streams of essential trade figures, and pink-haired Prellix draped over her guest chair.

"What are you doing HERE?" the Matriarch shouted. "What if he sees you? You should have vidded me." She did not like this woman.

"He won't come down here." Prellix sighed. "I heard the whole thing. He's enjoying the view and the coffee. Probably dreaming a little bit about what's under that business dress of yours."

"Stop it."

"My boss says you don't get to tell us to do things. It works the other way around or that little hideaway you have on Parthian Landing becomes a *much* more popular location." Prellix tilted her head, not looking at the Matriarch, as if she were daydreaming about a pleasant day far in the future. "For journalists, mostly."

"Yes, I know the data you have," the Matriarch snapped. "And I know it's verifiable. I verified it myself. Oh, thank goodness for a public verichain," she said sarcastically. "You don't really need to keep reminding me."

"And you don't really need to keep complaining about us." Prellix straightened herself up, put her feet on the floor, and leaned toward the Matriarch, who had taken a seat behind the desk. Somehow Prellix's short pink hair and all-leather outfit made it seem like she was behind the desk and the Matriarch was the guest.

"I just wanted to make sure you got him here. Which you did. And that you'll keep him here. Which you will. And that you'll authorize my people to make a little visit to the parking lot outside one of your lesser-used processing buildings. Savvy?"

"What's that mean?"

"*Savvy* means 'understand.' Do. You. Understand?" Prellix spoke slowly and abruptly as if the Matriarch were a child.

"Yes." The Matriarch sighed, deciding not to antagonize the dangerous brat.

"So?" Prellix waved her hands.

"Give me their names," the Matriarch said. "And IDs."

"They don't have IDs. Their names are Paul."

"Your people are all named Paul?"

"No, there's only one besides me and his name is Paul." Prellix seemed a little put out admitting this.

"I thought you said 'people,' that's all," the Matriarch muttered.

"I'll be there too," Prellix nagged.

The Matriarch scowled. "Are you sure you're up to this? That ship looked pretty complex."

"Not for you to worry about. Just get us in."

"Fine. But I also have to get someone to do a records search first."

"Uh-uh! No. Us first. Then your records search."

"He'll start to get suspicious if I'm gone too long."

"Why?" Prellix scoffed. "You're the Matriarch of Trade. He's more perplexed—if he's perplexed—that you're spending any time with him at all. Your absence will reassure him that you have only a passing interest. So . . ." Prellix smirked again, standing up so she towered over the Matriarch. "Take your time."

"Paul and Prellix Scalgote." The Matriarch sighed again and began adding them to an authorized list to enter the processing center where Pilot X's ship was parked.

HELP

"I'M SO SORRY that took so long," the Matriarch sang, accompanied by an implausibly skinny man in what looked to Pilot X like a stovepipe hat and a red dressing gown. "There are always a million things battling for my attention. Thank goodness I have Steiv." She patted the man on his shoulder.

"Steve?" said Pilot X.

"No, Steiv," said the Matriarch

"I like your hat," Pilot X said.

"Thank you," said Steiv. "It is a traditional Parthian Caravanners hat."

"Steiv is a bit of an iconoclast," the Matriarch said. "And a history buff. You romanticize preindustrial trading too much though, Steiv," she gently chided. It was obviously a well-worn argument between them.

"I do." He shrugged. "But I also do records searches, and our Lady says you require such?"

"She is correct," Pilot X said. "Did you want something to drink first? Coffee?" Pilot X asked.

The Matriarch and Steiv looked taken aback. Pilot X quickly got the idea that it was rude for him to offer a drink to the Matriarch's servant in the Matriarch's outdoor rooftop office in front of the Matriarch.

"I'm so sorry," he said. "I'm all out of sorts after the travel. But I've had coffee, so there's really no excuse."

The joke seemed to work. The Matriarch laughed and Steiv smiled.

"Let me give you the list." Pilot X began to read the names of the parts Verity had sent. Steiv didn't miss a beat, recording them into an air tablet. It was sort of a long, thin round stick that projected a full screen in the air.

Verity's last message to Pilot X noted that the list he was reading out was incomplete on purpose, as a safety measure. Verity worried they might put together what the parts were meant for if Pilot X handed over the complete list. Her message ended with the number 31 percent, which Pilot X knew meant there was a 31-percent chance they would still guess what the parts did.

"I'll get right on tracking these, though it may take some time depending on the supply chains," Steiv said when they were done.

"Of course. And thank you so much." Here Pilot X looked at the Matriarch, not Steiv, hoping to repair some of his missteps from earlier. She smiled graciously, and he got the idea that it helped.

"It is our pleasure," she said.

Without another word, Steiv left them.

"Well, I should really get back to my ship and do some maintenance. It's probably best if I stay there as well," said Pilot X.

"Nonsense," the Matriarch said. "You shall stay here with us. We have living quarters for guests in the building. They're quite comfortable. Some of our highest-level trading representatives stay there."

This shook Pilot X out of his coffee- and-architecture-induced sense of well-being. He was getting the feeling he was very gently being made a prisoner. "Matriarch, I couldn't," he objected. "It wouldn't be right. You've been too kind already."

"Your Bentrian modesty betrays you," she said. Which sounded odd to Pilot X, since Bentria wasn't a real place.

"And my maintenance," he insisted. "It really can only be done by me."

"Of course." The Matriarch nodded, looking suddenly distracted, as if someone were talking in her ear, which likely someone was. "I'll send you back by car." She collected herself, the voice apparently having stopped. "But won't you dine with me first? Your travels have been long and all you've had is coffee," she said, almost pouting.

She may have meant the bit about the car, in which case he should take her offer and get out of there. But if it was her car, would they really take him back? He decided if he went with her, he'd probably avoid being actually imprisoned for a little longer and possibly get to the bottom of what she was after for real. Besides, dinner might disarm her enough to reveal a few more clues before he returned to Verity. If he could return to Verity. Plus, he was hungry.

"How can I resist?" he said, throwing up his arms.

"Excellent. My favorite restaurant is on the next island over. It doesn't take but a moment to get there. I'll call for the car now. You wait here."

Before he could object, she rushed out, leaving him with the motionless bartender.

Pilot X wandered over and leaned against the bar. "Come here often?" he asked.

"Six days a week when not in maintenance mode," the bartender said.

INTRUDERS

SOFT, ALMOST FESTIVE lights bathed the gray parking lot where Verity was parked. She was watching two intruders. She knew they were intruders by their movements. They had authorization to enter but didn't act like it. They also very obviously were waiting to make sure no actual authorized personnel were around before they did whatever it was they came here to do. Also, they were wearing rather cheap masks.

To pass the time while Pilot X drank coffee and flirted with the Matriarch of Trade, Verity calculated the most likely reasons for the two intruders' behavior.

There was a 3-percent chance that it was just for fun. They weren't supposed to be there but wanted to see if they could get away with it. Thrill-seekers.

There was a 4-percent chance they believed they had a legitimate reason but someone else had been blocking them from it. Maybe there was some of their personal property in the processing building or one of the few other parked ships.

There was a 7-percent chance they wanted to break into the processing center to take something valuable, whether data or . . . Verity was fairly certain there wasn't much valuable in the processing center besides data.

There was a 19-percent chance they wanted to break into one of the other ships parked here and steal from it or steal it.

There was a 67-percent chance they wanted to steal her.

This wasn't arrogance on Verity's part. She was fairly sure she wasn't capable of arrogance. She was the most unusual ship in the yard. She would bring a big payoff to whomever took her. Even if they didn't come here intending to steal her, they would be tempted once they got a look at her.

Verity wasn't capable of feeling bad for thieves or anyone else, but she calculated that were she capable of such feelings, she might have felt bad for them. They had no idea what they were up against.

The two thieves decided that the coast was clear and made a beeline for Verity. It wasn't sneaky. They very obviously did not know Verity had intelligent surveillance. Which was unexpected. This was a trade civilization at its height. Certainly, ships in this era and place had intelligent surveillance. And she was obviously a unique ship, which made it likely she would have advanced systems. The thieves must not be very smart.

So Verity decided to take a direct approach, and used her external speakers. "Attention, approaching thieves. This ship is protected by multiple anti-theft protocols and an intelligent observation system. Please cease advancing and state your intentions."

"I thought you said he was gone, Prellix," Paul said.

"He is gone, Paul. That's a recording," said Prellix.

"Well, it saw us. Should we go? It probably has us recorded. We should go."

"We're wearing masks for a reason. Anyway, we'll wipe the recordings when we steal the ship."

"You will not be stealing the ship," Verity said, to make sure they understood she could hear them. "I have alerted my pilot and he will arrive shortly. I have also alerted the law enforcement agencies, who will be here shortly. Please disperse."

"We'd better go," said Paul.

"It's a recording, Paul. Just shut up and help me." Prellix began setting out silver cylinders at equal lengths in a circle around Verity. Paul began to do something with the wires that connected them. Verity had never observed such a series of devices before, but she assumed it was meant to disrupt her sensors and somehow overload her systems and unlock the hatches.

"That won't work. My systems are hardened against EM pulses, all known forms of radiation, and psychotronic-wave hacking, among other things."

"OK, Prellix, how did it know that if it's a recording?"

"It's guessing. It'd say the same thing no matter who approached it," she said, sounding just a tiny bit less sure.

"I'm not guessing," Verity said.

"What if it's got one of those artful intelligents?" Paul said.

"Yes. I am an artificial intelligence," said Verity.

"You won't find AI on a ship this small," said Prellix, very much trying to convince herself.

"Then how did it know I said that?" Paul insisted, stopping work on the wires.

"Because I can hear and understand you," said Verity.

"Paul! Just keep working it. It's obviously got some rudimentary speech recognition, OK?"

"Prellix. Paul. Please stop what you're doing immediately. I see you are trying to create some sort of net out of wires and cylinders that will attempt to bypass my security. It will not work. Please take off your orange masks and return to your homes," Verity tried.

Paul threw his hands up. "That's it! It definitely knows we're here. It knows our names! It can see our masks!"

"So. What?!" yelled Prellix. "We can still shut it down and steal it."

"No! It's too smart for us," Paul whined, but picked up a wire again.

"Too smart for you, you mean," Prellix snapped, and kept working.

Verity gave up being nice and sent out a shock pulse that fried the cylinders. Paul dropped the wires and fell back, shaking his hands. Prellix dropped the cylinder she had been holding and said, "Ow."

"I have overloaded your net device," said Verity. "Please leave."

Prellix stopped and looked at the ship. "Maybe you're right, Paul."

"Yeah, we should go."

"No, about the AI. You *are* an AI, aren't you?"

Paul started to answer, but Prellix shushed him without looking at him.

"What is your name, AI?" Prellix addressed Verity.

"Verity."

"Verity, what is fifteen divided by zero?"

Verity imitated a sigh. "Infinity."

"All people named Prellix are liars," said Prellix.

"Good to know," said Verity.

"Seretel is a man. All men are mortal—"

Verity had to interrupt her. "I won't have trouble with logic bombs or the like."

"Convince me you're intelligent," said Prellix.

"I see no reason to do that."

"If you do, we'll go," said Prellix.

"You should go anyway. The law officials are almost here."

A siren blared nearby.

Paul went white. "Prellix, we have to go."

"Fine," said Prellix. "But this is not the last you'll see of us, Verity. Or at least of me." She gathered the wires and burnt cylinders and put them back into the bag.

Paul and Prellix ran out of the yard and Verity watched them go. She marveled at the coincidence of the siren. Verity had not called the police or contacted Pilot X. She had been confident she could scare off the thieves without them. She had been right.

DINNER

THE NEXT ISLAND over was not far by distance, but it did take a while to fly there, and the Matriarch was busy with work for most of the journey. There was nothing to see out the window but the planet's vast expanse of ice-blue water. He couldn't even see the sun from his seat, since it was behind them. He tried to entertain himself by surreptitiously typing out a message to Verity asking if an AI could get bored, but she only responded that she was busy. She really had mastered lying. What could she possibly be busy with?

He ended up pulling out a screen from one of the seat pockets. It was filled with games, local video entertainment, and a few books. He read an article about Parthian Prime's hottest nightclubs. Then he played a puzzle game that required you to match three sea creatures called Lemians. They looked like turtles with wings. He assumed those were swimming limbs of some sort.

He was about to choose a video recounting the adventurous days of the early Parthian trade pioneers when the Matriarch put down her work, sighed, and stretched, leaning back and raising her arms high above her head. "Oh, thank you, Pilot X, for giving me an excuse to get away. I do love my work, but it can be tiring all the same. I need reasons to interrupt it sometimes and I don't always find the justifications. You are a most pleasant justification." She lowered her arms but stayed leaning back, smiling, her eyes half closed.

"Happy to oblige," he said, trying to resist the temptation to demand they take him back to Verity immediately. His gut told him he had to stick this out.

They landed in a smaller city than Parthian Prime. The tall buildings were concentrated around white sand beaches and filled with people enjoying themselves.

"This is Leegoes," said the Matriarch. "It's one of our most popular destinations because it's such a short hop from the capital. People from off planet or even the other side of the planet have to wait years to get a booking. But as a Parthian Prime permanent resident, I'm allowed to access the island anytime I want. And as Matriarch of Trade, I can get a table at any restaurant I want. And I want to get a table at Rix."

"Rix?" Pilot X said, trying to express polite interest.

"My favorite restaurant ever. They serve the most delightful meals. Always different and often foreign. I wouldn't even be surprised if they had this 'pie' you were asking about."

Pilot X didn't get his hopes up.

Rix was, in fact, gorgeous. It was set right on the beach, and every table had a view of the water. The menu, however, was rather traditional in Pilot X's opinion. It had multiple kinds of fish, the pictures showing ordinary types and preparations. They served some bird and other animal meats in rather typical styles. It all looked good, just not unusual to Pilot X.

"Oh, I'm so excited!" the Matriarch said. "They have shiggen with pineapple."

On the menu, Pilot X saw what looked to him like a brown chicken breast sitting under a pineapple circle. He was about to ask about the Pineapple Planet—he still hadn't ascertained its survival—when the waiter arrived.

"Welcome back to Rix, Matriarch. It is so good to see you."

"Thank you, Gazdun. So nice of you to remember me. This is my guest, Pilot X."

"Mr. X, welcome to Rix. We're glad to have you." Pilot X smiled, ignoring the insult, since nobody left in existence knew it was rude to call an Alendan by just a last name or to add an improper title.

"He comes from a very interesting planet called Bentria," the Matriarch gushed. "They don't use titles there. Pilot X is his name and in fact the politest way to refer to him, do I have that right?"

Pilot X just nodded, marveling that the Matriarch had remembered that detail. Maybe there was some sincerity to her after all. So, make that two people in existence who knew the rules of Alendan title courtesy. Three, if Gazdun remembered it.

"My apologies, Pilot X," said Gazdun.

"Not at all," said Pilot X. "So, what's good?"

"Well, the Matriarch is a big fan of the shiggen and I noticed you looking at the pineapple special we have on the menu today." The Matriarch giggled as if he'd caught her doing something very naughty. Pilot X briefly wondered what kind of relationship Gazdun and the Matriarch actually had. "Do you have a favorite type of protein?" Gazdun asked.

"Any kind full of amino acids works for me usually." Pilot X smiled. Gazdun and the Matriarch did not react. "Or fish?" Gazdun at least nodded at that. "Fishy fish," Pilot X continued. "I like my fish quite fishy." He was regretting agreeing to this now. And yet he was hungry and still curious about the Matriarch.

Gazdun interrupted this. "The zaban might be to your liking. It's caught in the southern waters off Galliol and flown in fresh daily. It's prepared with salt and teckwanna sauce."

Pilot X bravely ordered it without even bothering to find out what teckwanna sauce was.

"Excellent," the Matriarch said. "And bring us some springy rolls, too."

"Already on the way, as is your usual bottle of legwas."

No sooner had Gazdun turned to leave than a small army of waitstaff were covering the table with bread, a bottle of what Pilot X could only guess was legwas, set in a cooler, new glasses, new plates, seven kinds of sauces, and a pile of what looked like salt but smelled vaguely of flowers.

One of the waitstaff army poured the Matriarch some legwas: she tasted it, moaned something that must have meant it was acceptable, and both glasses were filled. When the waitstaff platoon melted away, the Matriarch raised a glass.

"To trade," she said.

"To trade," Pilot X imitated. He was about to clink the glass, but the Matriarch was already drinking.

She launched into a monologue describing Parthian Prime's unique trading advantages that contributed to its position at the top of the trading universe. Pilot X tried very hard not to drift. The coffee was wearing off and the legwas was quite strong. Or maybe that's just what legwas was supposed to be like. Or she had drugged him. He distracted himself from that thought by paying attention to how elegantly the Matriarch skirted the issue of Parthian Prime's claim as the original planet of the civilization. Certain omissions in her monologue implied there was only one answer to the origin of Parthians, but she was never so blunt as to say it.

She was describing their "original place as the heart of trade for our people" when the main course arrived. The conversation became slightly less one-sided, since the Matriarch was careful not to talk with food in her mouth. Pilot X was finally able to ask a few questions. Nothing too prying to start, just where she came from and where she went to school. Loosening her up.

It turned out Parthian Prime did not have anything like school. The Matriarch asked him to explain what school was like for him. "In Al—" He almost said Alendan. "In our society," he recovered, "we train for a purpose, get tested, and graduate into that field of work. In my case, I went to flight school, passed the final flight test, and became a t—" He stopped himself from saying *timeship*. "Trade pilot." *Nice save*, he congratulated himself.

"Oh heavens, that seems so odd to me." She laughed. "Though I know it's so common." Which made Pilot X wonder why she had forced him to explain it. "Here we just know from youth what we will be, and we begin working in that field. Occasionally someone will 'jump,' as we call it, and there's no shame in it. There are always transferable talents. But I'd say more than three quarters of people stay in the field they begin in at birth."

Pilot X almost spit out some legwas. "Birth?"

"Oh, it's a figure of speech. It's not as dreary as it sounds," the Matriarch objected. "The categories for infants are quite broad. Object-oriented, sound-oriented, things like that. Then as you grow and show predilections for certain things, say math, or language, you get subdivided more until by your teen years you're pretty settled into an occupational track. Specialization doesn't come until you're ready. And"—she shrugged—"it's always hard to explain this to outsiders, but you always know. Everybody knows. It just becomes obvious that you are a coder or a home designer or—"

"A Matriarch of Trade," offered Pilot X.

"HA!" She spit out a little legwas herself. "No, no, it's not quite THAT specific. Or easy. No, I was routed into trade ministration to be sure, but I had to earn respect and, of course, election to get where I am."

"Do you ever wish you'd left Parthian Prime?"

"Oh, I've left many times. I've visited many planets," she said, swirling her legwas.

"No, I mean left to work elsewhere. Do something else."

She scowled. She had the look again like someone was talking in her ear. "Oh no. No. I love it here. I truly do." But she kept scowling. "I'm sorry, Pilot X, but there's an urgent call I'm afraid I'll have to take. I'll return as soon as I can. Go ahead and order dessert. Gazdun knows what I like."

She got up, distracted, and wandered off through the restaurant and out of sight.

Pilot X ordered three desserts. "Just in case we have last-minute guests," he told Gazdun. He hoped one of the orders would accidentally turn out to be pie. His hopes would not be fulfilled.

SUSPICIOUS

AN ALERT IN the Matriarch's holoview told her to contact Prellix. She tried not to look annoyed as she rushed to find a secluded section of the restaurant to make the call. The nerve of this woman. If she didn't have such damning information, the Matriarch could have dealt with her easily. And permanently.

The Matriarch ended up in a decorative garden that was never used outside the rear of the restaurant, away from the beach. As soon as Prellix was on the line, the Matriarch said, "I'm in the middle of distracting him right now. Getting called away is suspicious and not helping."

"His ship's security system is more sophisticated than we expected," Prellix said, ignoring her. "We need you to get him off Parthian Prime."

"Just get him when he returns back to his ship tonight," said the Matriarch, wanting to be done with the whole mess. She was tired of being blackmailed. She was tired of being worried. She was growing tired of pretending to like Pilot X and she was very tired of talking to this pink-haired incompetent. Couldn't someone sophisticated enough to dig up deeply hidden dirt on the Matriarch hire better people? Were they not from this universe?

Prellix was droning on. "If we get arrested trying to kidnap him, do you think that would persuade us to be more likely or less likely to release the information we have?"

"What do you want me to do about it?" the Matriarch said, ignoring the threat.

"You haven't given him the trace on the parts yet, have you?"

"No."

"What did you plan to give him?"

"Whatever Steiv finds, to be honest. I didn't think it would matter. If you cared about him finding the parts, you should have said."

"We don't care about him finding the parts. We figured we'd have his ship by now and that would be the end of it. I need you to send him somewhere sparsely inhabited. It can't be uninhabited; that's too suspicious. I need him to go somewhere he'll try to land. But it needs to be primitive, so they won't care, or even know, if we attack him in orbit. I need—"

"You need me to come up with a good place for you to hijack him?" the Matriarch offered.

"Yes. Where is that?" Prellix said.

The Matriarch sighed. "Sending you the coordinates now."

She ended the call to Prellix and immediately contacted Steiv. Like a good ministry up-and-comer, he was promptly available, though it looked as if he were dressed to stay in for the night. Was that a bathrobe?

"Steiv! Sorry to bother you, dear, but I'm getting some pressure to finish up with Pilot X. How close are we with that trace?"

"Almost done. I have about half the parts nailed down. Just waiting for the others to corroborate. It's the weirdest route. Very circular. You should have the documentation first thing in the morning."

"Excellent. Slight request. Send all the locational information to me in a separate packet from the personal details. I don't want those mixed. Clearer for navigation that way. I'll sign off on them before you hand them over."

"OK." Steiv paused. "What about verification codes? Those would be on both then. Redundant . . ." He trailed off.

"Doesn't matter. Just keep the packets separate. Good?" the Matriarch asked pointedly.

"No problem at all, Matriarch."

"Excellent. Have a great night," she said, almost adding "doing whatever you're doing," but thought better of it.

"Thank you, Matriarch. Good night."

RELIEVED

PILOT X HAD eaten one dessert and was most of the way through the second by the time the Matriarch returned.

She looked harried. "I'm so sorry, Pilot X. Trade never ceases, as they say. And I see you made yourself at home." She smirked. It was the first honest expression Pilot X thought he had seen from her. It also made him a touch sad. In the back of his mind he had hoped her interest in him was genuine. Not that he was looking for interest. Not yet. Maybe not ever. Certainly not from the Matriarch. He suspected his heart had been destroyed with Alexandra and the rest of Alenda. But the idea that maybe he could spark interest gave him the idea that a shard of his heart might have survived after all.

But no. The heart was not involved in this relationship. Which left him still wondering about the real reason she was feigning interest in him. He should have Verity run a probability table on it.

"None of these are pie, but what I've had is delicious," Pilot X said between mouthfuls of something chocolaty and creamy. He had finished off the sticky bowl of something fruity. The sour-smelling bowl of something green waited in front of the Matriarch's seat.

"Gazdun said you'd like . . . that." Pilot X motioned at the bowl of green with his spoon.

"Oh yes, Crème de Real. It's a dish that originated on Parthian Real. I know it looks like bad soup, but it tastes like heaven." She ate a spoonful and her eyes rolled back in her head and a low murmur escaped as she closed her eyes. Pilot X thought it must have been what he looked like when he ate pie. That made him sad.

"Well, the good news from my delay is that I talked to Steiv. He'll have your parts trace ready for you in the morning. Where are you planning to stay?"

Her gazed lingered on him in a way that he was fairly certain was meant to imply an invitation, which should have opened a whole evening of will-they-won't-they fun and games. But he knew they would end up going nowhere, or if they did go somewhere, it would probably be somewhere both would regret.

"On my ship. I'm pretty comfortable there," he said. This would sound like he was used to roughing it, because the Matriarch didn't know he had a five-point adjustable supercomfort mattress on a spring-loaded, gimball-activated Alendan bed. They literally did not make them like that anymore. Because all the Alendan bed-makers no longer existed. Now he was really sad. He just wanted to go.

"Well, you wouldn't have to—" she teased.

"Nope. Ship's fine. Wouldn't want to put you out. So, tell me more about the green soup?" He waved his spoon at the Crème de Real.

He thought she looked relieved. "It's made from the sap of a friezewood tree. They used to only exist on Parthian Real and the best ones still do. . ." She kept explaining, but Pilot X let the words wash over and soothe him. He held his head as if listening but let his gaze focus past her on the slowly rolling waves. He put his guilt out on the waves and tried to let the sea take it away. It bobbed and drifted and every time he thought it had floated away, the tide or the wind pushed it back within sight.

"Do you have anything like that in Bentria?" the Matriarch was asking.

"Like what?" Pilot X asked.

"Song Crème." She smiled, probably guessing that he hadn't been listening.

"Oh no. We have almost no creams at all," he answered truthfully. Since Bentria didn't exist, it really had nothing, not even cream.

DETAILS

"HONEY, I'M HOME," Pilot X said as he sat down in the cockpit.

"How was your dinner?" Verity asked.

"Slightly delicious with somewhat interesting but ultimately disappointing desserts and lackluster conversation. I mostly went there for the waters. There were waters there. I was not misinformed. How were things with you?"

"Mostly the same. Except for when two people named Prellix and Paul tried to steal me."

"Well, I'm sorry to hear tha—say that again? Someone tried to steal you? What?"

"Yes, I was able to convince them not to and they left."

"Tell me a little more."

Verity told him all the details.

"Well, that explains it," he said.

"Explains what?" asked Verity.

"Why the Matriarch was so flirty."

"Was she?"

"She was. And it seems she has designs on my—you. But she says she has the information on the parts we need, which she'll get to us tomorrow morning. So, either she's delaying us to try to make another attempt to steal you, or she gave up and will give us the parts info. If we're lucky, we get out of here with some intel and ourselves. If not, we may have to hustle and leave empty-handed."

"We should leave now," Verity said.

Leaving without the parts info would be a defeat that he could not deal with right now. The hope of that info was the only thread of purpose he had at the moment. Didn't she know that? "That'd be rude," he said. "And would make me regret leaving my hut. We need to know where those parts came from."

"The chances of any intel being actually delivered are 12.8 percent. The chances that we will get any useful intel are . . . smaller."

"You're getting better at those generalizations. But it doesn't matter. Even if it's mostly lies, we might find a few truths and that'll be progress. We wait."

"In that case, the supercomfort is prepared for you with fresh sheets."

"Take me to bed, Verity."

NOODLES

PRELLIX SAT PRECARIOUSLY on a much-too-small stool in a small, ugly street-side stall in Parthian Prime, slurping noodles that tasted like rain and cat guts. It was the flavor she'd ordered for Paul, but they had given her two by mistake.

"Vagson. Looks like a hellhole," she said, exploring the coordinates the Matriarch had sent.

"I don't see how moving to a primitive planet is going to get us past the security system," Paul said, hungrily eating his noodles.

"It won't. But it will let us put a gun to the pilot's head and make him deactivate the ship and transfer ownership to us. That's what we want."

"What if the AI doesn't want to transfer?"

"That'sh not how it worksh," she said, forcing down a mouthful of noodles. "It does what its owner tells it. It has to. We attack it and force him to order it to transfer, or he dies. He orders the AI to obey a new master and it'll all be good. You with me?"

"I'm always with you," said Paul.

The usually subservient or fearful Paul said this with an unusual amount of dissatisfaction. Prellix actually looked at him. He wasn't mad. He just looked dejected.

She couldn't have that. As bad as he was at everything, she still needed him at times. She breathed in. "Hey. I'm with you too," Prellix said. "That's why I ordered you your favorite flavor." She gently punched him on the shoulder.

A smile worked its way out of the dejected look. "Thanks, sis," Paul said.

ANSWERS

THE NEXT MORNING Pilot X was up and headed to the processing building to see if there was more coffee, but he ran into Steiv first.

"Good morning, Pilot X. I have the data you requested."

"Excellent! Come with me to get some coffee," Pilot X said.

Steiv didn't move, just held out a large silver package. "I wish I could," he said without smiling or in any other way indicating he wished he could, "but I must attend to other business. The Matriarch bids you well and thanks you for your company." Steiv gave a short bow and turned to go. Pilot X continued toward the processing center, but Steiv called after him.

"Oh, Pilot X. I hate to say this," he said, smiling, "but the processing center is most likely locked. And your landing permit expires shortly. It's all in the documentation. You may want to look it over soon." Steiv left without waiting for a reaction.

Pilot X finished walking over to the building anyway, but it was in fact locked. He stomped back to Verity. As he entered the ship, he smelled something impossible.

"Is that coffee?"

"Yes. I was able to place an order on the local subnet for a small delivery. I'm afraid it's just enough for today, since we didn't have any credits. I could only get a free-trial sample delivered."

"Verity, you're amazing."

Pilot X poured a cup and sat down in his pilot's chair to look over the documentation.

It was a folder made of a very thin, slick silver substance, possibly some kind of plastic. Inside were hard copies of destination reports and summaries of the parts delivery history. A thin data module in a format Pilot X didn't recognize was also tucked into the folder. He held up the data module. "Can you read this?" he asked.

"Possibly. Place it in the universal reader and I'll do my best."

While Verity worked on that, Pilot X paged through the slim plastic hard copies. He assumed that they assumed he wouldn't easily be able to read the module, so it was nice of them to give him these. Well, *nice* was a strong word for what was probably motivated by the desire to delay him so they could try to steal the ship. He put the paper he was looking at down. But then why would Steiv try to rush them off the planet? If the Matriarch was trying to steal Verity—was it a trap? Would they be attacked in space as they departed?

He decided it didn't matter. Let them try. Nobody could match Verity in this universe. What mattered was whether this info was good. And why wouldn't it be? Even if they wanted to steal Verity, it would be easier to give him real data than waste time faking it. Which meant he would find out where these parts were going so they could find and stop the person who was trying to re-create the Instant.

"Where's Vagson?" Pilot X asked.

"It's not far from here. It orbits an early stage star and does not exit industrial production before social collapse. Or"— Verity made an unusual pause that sounded like uncertainty—"that information was taken from my own pre-Instant records and may not match with this universe. I cannot verify it with public information on the Parthian subnet."

"It's not listed?"

"Vagson is listed, but there is not much detail."

"What does it say?"

"Vagson. Fourth planet in young star system. Primitive. No trade value. No outside contact."

"You're not kidding; that isn't much."

"Meanwhile, the data disk they gave us about the parts is going to take—a considerable amount of time to read. Shall I continue working on it?"

"Yeah, go ahead, but you can make it low priority. I have almost everything we need here in the hard copies. I guess we're headed to Vagson. If this is a no-contact planet, then anyone visiting would have to go undercover. If you don't, people find out really fast. The only way that makes any sense is if the parts were being laundered."

"Vagson does not seem like the first choice for cleaning parts."

"Not that kind of laundered—was that a joke?"

Verity paused for a fraction longer than usual. "No."

Pilot X wondered if Verity was developing the ability to be embarrassed but decided that if she was, it would be embarrassing to call attention to it. "I meant, the parts were routed through Vagson to hide where they were really going. Which is odd, because Parthians would suspect that just like I would. You'd think they'd investigate that."

"Or the Matriarch is lying and this data is not valid," Verity suggested cheerfully.

Pilot X thought about it. "Either way, there's one way to find out. The Matriarch may try to steal you again. Are you prepared for that?"

"As I believe I showed last night, I am always adequately prepared."

Pilot X couldn't argue with that. "So, on to Vagson then. When should we arrive?" Pilot X asked.

"Since the Parthians do not have time travel, I assumed we would travel there in adjusted real time." Adjusted real time meant only using time travel to wipe out the length of the journey. Essentially, they would aim to arrive not long after they left.

"Hmmm. That makes sense if we just want to get to the parts, but I'd kind of like to get the lay of the land. Do a little discreet observation. Maybe a year before we leave here, relatively speaking of course? Do a little research then jump to current time? That way the Matriarch can't warn them."

"That is an acceptable plan variation," Verity said.

"You're slipping."

"Slipping?"

"Not funny and not very natural."

"You should know," Verity said.

Pilot X wasn't even sure what to make of that. "Let's just go," he said.

FIRST ATTEMPT

SHE WAS SURE it was ready. The order would be pleased with this. Sort of. Only because she had asked so much and they would want to see a result. This was her project.

But she needed them to continue to give her privacy, resources, and cover stories. And they had not been pleased about her requests to route parts through Parthian Prime. One hundred and fifty messages containing requests, forms, counter-requests, and "cross-disciplinary provisional dispensations." Two of those messages actually approved anything. An actual bureaucratic nightmare would have seemed like a pleasant break from the reality. She could not stomach trying to navigate that mess again, much less the need to convince the Order to let her. So this was it.

The lights glowed, providing no heat but still making her feel warm inside. The fans hummed like a musical prelude. The switch on the Time Rip Regenerator seemed to beckon her to start the test. She would not activate the main ripeon tuner this time. It lay cold and uninvolved, cut off from the rest of the chain of parts. This would just send out coordinated test waves.

She bit her lip, looked skyward, and flicked the switch.

Was it her imagination? Did the room shimmer? Or was that just her anticipation?

She rushed forward to the screen that showed the test readings.

All tests but one showed red. She had generated ripeons but not in any coordinated way. The test waves just randomly shot out in a roughly cone-like shape useful for nothing she wanted to do.

She slumped.

She would start again tomorrow. She had been working for twenty-eight hours on this. She needed to clear her mind.

Just then there was a knock at the door. She jumped. The disappointment in her chest sank into her gut and became worry. She had strict orders never to be disturbed. Well, almost never.

She opened the door a crack. Outside was the old man.

"Your boss wants to see you," he said, then walked back down the hall.

She sighed. Then she followed him.

AGAIN

A METAL SHACK stood on an otherwise empty brown plain. Verity had identified this place as the source. Faster than he expected, he was at the door. He knocked, but no one answered. He tried the handle and it turned, creaking as it swung open without him trying.

It was dim inside, but he could see a bench with machine parts laid out on it. They were the parts for the Instant. They were laid out in an odd configuration. He couldn't quite put his finger on what was wrong, but he could tell it wasn't the way he had put it together. A switch was connected, though, and a light indicated power was flowing. He needed to undo this immediately.

He followed a cable from the switch to where it connected to one of the parts, and began to unscrew the cable's connector. Then he stopped. He didn't know this system. Disconnecting the switch could accidentally trigger it. He needed to disconnect the power first. He searched and found a battery. He turned off the power compartment then removed the battery.

"What are you doing?"

He knew that voice.

He turned to find Alexandra.

"What are you doing, my love?" She smiled. His heart sang. He could see nothing but that smile.

He rushed to her, his heart bursting. She laughed as he grabbed her, and she leaned in for a long-imagined, impossible kiss. Time became irrelevant.

"How did you get here?" he finally asked, gasping.

"I've always been here." She smiled again. "Working on this."

She left his embrace, despite his attempt to hold on, and moved over to the table. "Why did you take out the battery?" She furrowed her brow but without dropping her smile.

"We have to stop it," he said.

She tilted her head and looked concerned, though still smiling. "No, my love. This is how I return to you. I need to reset things so we can be together."

"What? No!"

The smile dropped into a frown. "Do you not want to be together?"

"No, I mean yes, but not that way. It won't work."

"But we have to try!" she pleaded, moving back toward him and grabbing him by the arms. It was gentle, but it also hurt.

He shook his head. "No, my love. If you use this again, it will erase billions. And—and it won't bring you back."

"Might not," she teased. "And if it doesn't, we just try again. And again. And again." She let go of him and picked up the battery to put it back in.

He was horrified. "Alexandra, no! We can't do that to the universe. I can't live with doing it once. I could never—"

"We've already done it," she said, her back turned but her hand on the switch.

Pilot X screamed.

Alexandra turned. "We've arrived," she said in a flat, emotionless voice.

"What?!" Pilot X screamed.

"We've arrived," Verity said.

Pilot X jumped awake in the cockpit chair.

"We've arrived at the Vagson System. I hope you slept well," said Verity.

VAGSON

VERITY BROUGHT THEM into the Vagson system above the ecliptic, so they could get a good look around. She could jump them in closer whenever they wanted.

The system had a very young star and eleven planets. The inner four were rocky, with one dual-planetary system. There was debris where a fifth rocky planet had been then, and there were five gas giants and two outer rocky planets, both dual.

"Reminds me of one from the war," Pilot X said quietly.

Verity jumped them into orbit around the fourth planet. It had a thin atmosphere and was about 50 percent water. The land looked dry, with little green.

"This is where sentient life evolved? There're better options in the system."

"There is non-sentient life on two other planets and two other moons, but it is limited and shows no signs of pre-sentience."

"Vagson doesn't look very stable."

"It is not. Projections show it will lose its atmosphere within the next eight hundred years."

"Can we check?"

Verity moved them forward in time eight hundred years. The planet was dead below them, with almost no atmosphere and no sign of water.

"Did the sentient life go elsewhere? Wait, don't answer that. Just take us back."

"But I have already scanned and found—"

"Don't tell me. Take us back, Verity."

Verity moved them back to just after they had first arrived in the system, so they wouldn't overlap with themselves. Pilot X thought the planet didn't look much better, even with a full atmosphere and water. It looked sickly. He wanted to help them, which was why he hadn't let Verity tell him their fate. If he knew they didn't survive, he would either give up the idea or run up against all manner of paradox provisions. Granted, there were no Guardians of Alenda around to enforce restrictions like that, but it didn't make paradoxes any less real. The fact that he did not know their fate was essential, not just on an ethical level but on a physical one as well. He could act freely, and the universe would do what it would, but he wouldn't be pushing against it. And maybe he could fix them. He could fix someone. He could do something good in this new universe.

"I'm going to help them."

"You can't," Verity said.

"Why not?"

"The rule against non-interference?"

"The—you mean Article Sixteen of the Trevellian Code. The Second Phase Renderings of the Guardians of Alenda?" He couldn't believe she was bringing that up as a serious objection.

"Yes."

"Doesn't apply," he said, annoyed at her pouring water on his enthusiasm. Did she want him to just go back to the hut?

"I don't see how it doesn't apply," she said.

"Partly because this is a civilization in peril."

"That exception refers to peril of a nonnatural or non-evolutionary matter such as a Sensaurian attack."

"There's another reason though."

"What's the other reason?"

"Because I said so."

"Your saying so doesn't change the rule."

"Doesn't it?"

"It doesn't."

"But I'm the last of the Alendans. I'm all of the Alendans. I'm the entire Alendan civilization."

"But the rule remains."

"I declare the rule overturned." Pilot X smirked.

"Only the Guardians of Alenda in parliament assembled can amend the articles of any Phase of the Renderings," Verity answered.

That got him. Here he was again. The last of his kind with no support. No one like him to help him. His hut was calling. He almost gave up again, but the prospect of an extra layer of guilt layered around the huge pit of guilt he already carried stopped him. He couldn't go back. He had to fix things. And here was something he could fix. He knew it. He couldn't let laws from a universe that no longer existed stop him, even if his only friend had been programmed to remember all those laws and follow them strictly. Then he had an idea.

"We just need an election!" Pilot X snapped his fingers. "Remind me, do AI have the franchise?"

"AI do not have voting rights."

"Sad. Well, hold on." Pilot X took a sheet from the Parthian documents, found a marking device, and scribbled away. "Here. This is the new ballot for the election of parliament."

On the page he had written, *Ballot of officers of the Guardians of Alenda*, and had *Pilot X* listed next to a square. Pilot X made a great show of checking off the box.

"Would you like to count the votes? We need an independent observer," Pilot X said.

"This election is nonstandard—"

"Doesn't matter! I have the common-law right of the populace behind me that, in light of major catastrophes, ballot rules may be relaxed or modified if proper officers are absent, which they are. Now, what's the count?"

"Pilot X has a very low number of votes."

"Very funny. What's the EXACT count?"

"Pilot X has one vote."

"And what percentage is that?"

"One hundred percent."

"This election is certified! Fantastic. Now, as the only officer, I declare parliament in session. Your Honor? Yes, the chair recognizes Pilot X. Thank you, me. It is with great humbleness and largeness of pomposity and overwrought prose that I put before you today a most serious proposal to overturn and obliterate Article Sixteen of the Trevellian Code, the Second Phase Renderings of the Guardians of Alenda. May its provisions on non-interference particularly be considered null and void. What say you, Chair? I say we need to weigh expert opinions. Ah, a fair point! The Chair recognizes expert testimony from the AI Verity. Verity, what is your opinion on the proposal at hand?"

"You should not overturn the article."

"And why does such an esteemed and otherwise agreeable AI object?"

"Your pantomime of a parliament is entertaining but spurious. The article was enacted after thousands of years of experience and with the weight of multiple opinions and incidents behind it. It should not be overturned by one man on a whim."

"A compelling argument. Pilot X, what say you in answer?" Pilot X said to himself, then jumped across the cabin facing where he had just stood. "Your Honor, it is with the most fervent desire for gravity and judicious behavior that I am compelled to note that our language refutes this 'Verity's' judgment of us as frivolous. By syllabic count alone we believe we are shown to be not only anti-frivolous but downright sober. We move to carry the motion to overturn." Pilot X jumped again. "Voice vote. Say *aye* to overturn. Aye." He jumped and said "aye" as Verity said "nay."

Pilot X jumped back again and said, "Let the record show the only nay vote was from our expert witness, who is not a voting member of the parliament and therefore that vote cannot be counted. But even if it we counted it, the final vote is 2–1; the article is overturned." He jumped again and began clapping and shouting approval for himself.

"May I say one more thing?" Verity asked.

"The Chair recognizes the expert witness, the AI Verity, with a codicil to our proceedings."

"The rule existed to prevent the kinds of abuse that the Secretary perpetrated during the dimension war. Among his many reprehensible acts was the Manic Masters project, arming dictators of primitive societies in order to advance their technologies unnaturally. It was, as you said yourself, one of the cruelest maneuvers he made. Even if done for a good purpose, interfering and advancing technology may make things infinitely worse and could unleash something horrible that you cannot predict. To prevent such occurrences is why the article existed."

Verity was right. Pilot X had seen the devastation that the Secretary's Manic Masters program had caused as he tried to force civilizations to advance faster for his own purposes. It generally caused intense destruction and trauma in the originating systems and, only through sheer luck, did not result in something universally worse. Pilot X had erased that from history. He could not be the one to bring it back.

"The parliament moves to add a revised Article Sixteen saying no Alendan may artificially advance the technology of any species. All in favor? Aye." Verity did not speak this time. Pilot X did not jump. "I won't do that, Verity. You're right," Pilot X said, all the fervor and fun drained from him. "But I will try to warn these people on Vagson. They have eight hundred years. They might save themselves. And please don't tell me what will happen. I must do this. I must try to do good." He was saving himself as much as them.

Verity did not respond.

THE WISDOMER

PILOT X KNEW it was rude in most cultures to speak with one's mouth full of food.

"I'm so sorry, but this is just amazing, and I can't stop eating it." He smiled.

"It's quite all right." Jorendren, his host, laughed, shaking his long, lanky frame. The people of Vagson were another take on humanoids, reminding Pilot X that he needed to take some time to get Verity to look for signs of any non-humanoids in this new universe. Also, he needed to schedule a reminder to investigate the origins of humanoids. Another time.

For now, he continued the hunt. In this part of Vagson, people seemed to be split between short and squat folks who covered themselves with clothing so much that you couldn't tell what they looked like, and people who were long and lanky and wore scraps of denim in an odd collection that looked random but ended up covering all the things most cultures covered, with the hands and head exposed. Jorendren was decidedly this latter type, with a deep, dark blue outfit and tan leatherish shoes. Verity suspected the lanky ones must be descended from a people who evolved in lower gravity.

"I still can't believe you don't have gendran circles where you come from," Jorendren said, continuing to chuckle.

"We call it *pie*," said Pilot X. "But we ran out of it a long time ago."

"Pie." Jorendren laughed. "What an odd, short name."

Verity had wanted to scan for local officials and try to apply for information through the appropriate channels. That sounded like work to Pilot X. Throughout the entire dimensional war in his universe, he had been pulled into things without meaning to be. Now it had become his habit. He felt like if he let the universe—this new universe—tell him where to go, things would work out better than if he chose and was wrong. Verity did not like his approach, but so far it had resulted in him meeting the friendly Jorendren, who had offered to share his lunch, which turned out to be pie. As far as Pilot X was concerned, his approach was working.

"Gendrans are kind of like what we call *cherries*," he explained to Jorendren. "It's been a long time since I ate cherries."

"Well, I'm happy you like it. Gurnsey the baker will be proud. So don't fret. Eat up and talk. As the Wisdomer says, 'Full mouths make for happy hearts.'"

"An excellent phrase indeed," said Pilot X between bites of gendran circle. Or was this just a gendran triangle, since it was only a slice? He'd ask later. "So yes, I'm traveling around to share the findings of our scient—wisdomers?"

Now Jorendren looked a little shocked. "There is but one Wisdomer and she reigns in the moons now," he said solemnly.

"Well, what do you call smart people?" Pilot X asked. "People who study things and discover things?"

"Oh!" Jorendren brightened. "You mean sayers."

Pilot X was treading carefully. He had introduced himself to Jorendren as a traveler from a far-off land and was trying to get a handle on the local lingo. "I must mean sayers. Our sayers—we call them something else—have discovered some deep truths among the stars. They have bid me share these—sayings?—with others. But it is only one of my purposes in traveling here. For some of their instruments have been taken from them, so I seek them as well. I am, you might say, on a mission to find, as well as to give."

"I can introduce you to a sayer." Jorendren seemed proud of this. "She is well-known to me. I was just out here on the edge of town picking up some supplies for her, as a matter of fact. Come. I will take you to her. She lives here in Ladren."

Ladren was a city made of a collection of wooden structures, none more than three stories high. Verity estimated about three hundred thousand people lived there, but it was very dense. It was the largest city on the largest continent. Verity had insisted that if he was going to pursue his irrational approach that he at least pick a place with a lot of people, which would give him more opportunities for a random chance of success. Leave it to Verity to try to turn Pilot X's free-spirited approach into math.

As they walked, Pilot X noticed three men seemed to keep pace with them. He would have been nervous about this, but Jorendren paid them no mind. He assumed it was the normal way that crowds moved.

He should have been nervous.

At one point they turned to walk through a dim tunnel made by two three-story wood buildings, set close by the road with what looked like a crude scaffolding between them, covered in tarp.

"They're painting the guesteries," Jorendren was explaining, noticing Pilot X looking at the tarp overhead, when suddenly someone had grabbed his wrists and yanked him into what appeared to be an alley running off behind one of the buildings. Few people were in the tunnel, and they couldn't see far enough down the alley to notice.

Pilot X was forced to his knees by one of the lanky men who had been keeping pace. Another tall man had forced Jorendren to his knees. Jorendren whimpered, "Please don't take Lal's supplies."

"Lal?" said the third man, who was covered in rags. Rags of every color wound around him from head to toe, leaving openings for his feet, hands, and face. His feet were bare and dirty and his face and hands were too. "You're Jorendren of Nob then?"

Jorendren nodded.

"Stay quiet and still until we're done and we won't touch a hair on your head or a package in your sack."

Jorendren nodded again and added, "This man is our guest."

The raggedy man played with the ends of one of his rags. "See, I don't reckon that's exactly true. I saw this man walk into town alone. I saw you meet him like a stranger. All polite and bowing and such. And it may be true that you're taking him to Lal for an introduction. If that's the case, then he's not a guest yet. And Lal's not a warrior or the like, right? Mind, I don't like to be on Lal's bad side, but I don't expect to be—"

"You say a lot of things," Pilot X interrupted.

The lanky man holding him struck him in the head.

"And you just said a little too much." The raggedy man leaned down to stare at him. His breath smelled like fish. Fishy fish.

"Now. You came into our city, but you didn't pay the fee," the raggedy man said, straightening up.

"You gotta pay the fee," said the lanky man holding Jorendren.

"Fee's not optional," said the lanky man holding Pilot X.

"What's that?" said the raggedy man. He pointed at Pilot X's wrist where he wore the communication device for Verity.

"Looks like the fee to me," said the lanky man holding Pilot X.

"It does, don't it?" said the raggedy man.

"I think we have come to an equitable arrangement."

"Give the man his hand so he can pay his fee."

The lanky man let go of Pilot X's wrist. He thought about giving them the communicator. He had several more on the ship and Verity could disable it remotely as soon as she understood what had happened. Then he remembered her saying, *"Even if done for a good purpose, interfering and advancing technology may make things infinitely worse and could unleash something horrible that you cannot predict. To prevent such occurrences is why the article existed."*

Right. So he couldn't let them take it for their own good. Not a thing he could make them understand. So he punched the raggedy man.

It hurt. Pilot X didn't punch people.

"Oh no, stop," said Jorendren.

But in the follow-through of the punch, Pilot X had ended up standing above the raggedy man, who appeared to be out cold. Pilot X jumped to turn around. He tried not to show just how painful the ache in his hand was.

The lanky men had been about to grab him but stopped.

Suddenly a voice said, "The Wisdomer has ruled. Go now." It was a message from Verity amplified from the communicator.

The lanky men ran.

Jorendren looked at him in awe. "What—"

"It's a trick," Pilot X said quickly. "I just threw my voice." He tapped the communicator twice and added, "Jorendren, it was just"—and the words of—"a trick"—boomed out of the communicator as Pilot X stopped talking fast and mouthed them. "See?"

Jorendren scowled. "But impersonating the Wisdomer. I—"

Pilot X held up a hand. "I would never. I said, 'The Wisdomer has ruled,' didn't I?" He was almost sure that's what Verity had said. "And the Wisdomer forbids theft," Pilot X guessed.

Jorendren smiled. "I see. Clever. You are almost as clever as Lal. We should hurry so you can meet. I—" He looked at the raggedy man who was beginning to stir. "I don't know if your trick will last."

They left the alley and hurried on their way.

The sayer, called Lal, lived on the third floor above what Jorendren called a "steam shop" in one of many dense neighborhoods. The steam shop appeared to be just what it sounded like, with steam billowing out of several vents on two sides of a precarious two-story wooden building.

"All manner of methods happen in a steam shop," Jorendren said proudly. Jorendren seemed like the kind of person who took pride in being associated with other things. A kind of civic booster for Ladren. "There are machines that run on the steam. There are materials created by the steam. Some cooking can be done with the steam, though that's usually left for the steam-cookery purveyors."

He led Pilot X to a staircase that ran up the only side of the building without vents. It was crammed in a narrow gap between the steam shop and the next building. It was dark and moldy and Pilot X was unsure it would hold together, because both of them made it creak and sway on the way up to a bright copper door on the second floor. Jorendren rapped sharply on the door and shouted for Lal.

In the middle of his third knock, the door opened and a short, squat person appeared. Pilot X was fairly certain there was a person under all the garments. The person had a turban-like cloth wound around most of their head, such that it was impossible to tell if there was a face. Below that were what appeared to be several layers of robes all cinched about the middle with a broad leather belt. And where one might have expected boots, more cloth was wrapped around each leg, ending in some rather awkward-looking bunches down where feet might be expected.

"Oh, it's just Jorendren," the bundle said in a midrange squawk. "Did you get the sulfur powder I need?" Pilot X could see hints of a mouth under all the cloth bunched around the face.

"Yes, Lal. And I've brought a traveler from far—" Jorendren paused and looked at Pilot X, realizing he had never asked the name of his country.

"Alenda," Pilot X said truthfully.

"Yes, that's right. Of course. A traveler from the faraway land of Alenda, named Pilodix. He has traveled across the lands seeking certain—say, devices—that have been lost, and also wishes to share the sayings of his people with others."

It wasn't really what Pilot X had said at all, but it certainly gave him an insight into how the people of Ladren thought.

"You're a sayer?" the person squawked. This time Pilot X thought he caught a hint of green eyes above the mouth.

"I am what passes for that in my country," he said.

"Oh, don't start talking like Jorendren now. You're too dramatic, man! If I made any sense out of what he just said, it sounds like you lost some stuff and have some research you can share in exchange for information?"

Pilot X just nodded and smiled.

"And we were waylaid by Rel and his men. They tried to steal another of his say-devices but he—he was clever and stopped them."

"Humph. You don't say. Well, you better come on in. They shouldn't want to bother you once you're a guest. Unless you picked a fight with them." Pilot X wasn't sure if he should admit that was exactly what he'd done, so he said nothing.

Jorendren started to step through. "Not you, Jorendren! Make yourself useful and go get us a couple of bottles of garvee."

"Two?" Jorendren asked in the shortest sentence Pilot X had heard him speak.

"Fine, three. But you'll keep to yourself. Put it on my bill. Now go."

Jorendren took off back down the stairs in a hurry and the person inside the mound of rags motioned Pilot X to enter. Inside, it was dark and stuffy from the steam below and filled with several tables piled with paper and metal and glass devices in equal measure. A small path led through the tables to two chairs next to a lit fireplace.

"I'm Lal. What did he say your name was? Pidlysticks?"

"Pilot X."

"Pilod Ecksty. I'll just call you Pily. Never could get the hang of foreign names. Apologies. Have a seat."

The chair was insanely comfortable. The fire was not overly warm but incredibly cheering. He hoped garvee was coffee.

"What can I do for you, Pily? What's this stuff you're looking for?"

"They're scientific instruments. I have some descriptions of them if you'd care to look them over." He pulled out the hard copies he had gotten from Steiv. It was a good thing he had gotten hard copies, since this civilization had no electronics to speak of.

"What kind of paper is this? So slick. And what did you call them? Sybernific instruments?"

"Ah. Right. From what I can tell, you would call them sayer-devices?"

"Well, why didn't you say so? Yeah, I can see what you mean. These are fancy designs. I don't even know what half these words mean. You have some pretty high sayers over there in Belinda, it seems."

Pilot X didn't bother correcting that.

"Well, let's hear it," Lal said, leaning back. "No, wait. Let's wait for the garvee. Don't want you to get interrupted halfway through." Lal began to look around.

"What's garvee?" Pilot X asked.

"What's garvee?! What's GARVEE?! Pily, old buddy, you mean to tell me you've never had a good glass of garvee?! Well, we are about to fix your world."

Please let it be coffee please let it be coffee please let it be coffee.

"It is the purest nectar of the gods. Dark and brown and sweet."

Could be coffee. Coffee could be called brown. Maybe they sweeten it.

"Tastes like curling up by this fire and taking a nap. Always relaxes me."

Some people consider coffee relaxing.

"Doesn't make me sleep. Just mellows me out and so good tasting."

Pilot X drooped. "Oh. It sounds like beer."

"Beer," Lal sniffed. "Odd name for garvee."

Jorendren entered with three very large brown bottles. Lal got up and grabbed two glasses and a small folding table.

"Georder said, 'Tell Lal these are the last before her tab is settled,'" Jorendren said.

Lal sniffed at that too, otherwise ignoring Jorendren. She put the table down between the two chairs and dropped the glasses on top and, with the finish of the motion, grabbed the two bottles from Jorendren. "You won't need a glass," she said to him. "And drink it slow. You know how you get."

She popped the tops off the bottles and poured from each bottle into a separate glass. She picked up one of the glasses and handed it Pilot X, then picked up the other for herself.

"To the Wisdomer," said Lal.

"The Wisdomer," Jorendren said as Pilot X mumbled something so he appeared to participate.

"Now," Lal said, settling back into her seat. "Tell me your research. And Jorendren, stay quiet. I have a feeling I'll need to concentrate, give?"

Jorendren just nodded.

Lal nodded back and looked at Pilot X. He took a deep breath. If the parts were here on this primitive planet, he had to assume people like Lal would know. This society wouldn't know what they were. He guessed if they were here, they were hidden in exchange for knowledge, something scientists—or sayers—would always value. So that was his tactic too. He had plenty of knowledge to trade and, despite the Trevellian Code, nobody to stop him from trading it. His big gamble was to hope he could give them knowledge that would not interfere in their development but still lead to them saving their civilization. And at the end of that they'd find it worth enough to help him track down the parts.

"What do you call the star in the sky that moves and appears blue?" he asked.

"It's not a star, it's a planet. What kind of sayers do you have in Belinda?" said Lal. "We call it Merva, after the goddess of gems and stones. Everybody thinks it's a big topaz. Ridiculous. It's made of water. Probably a bunch of smart porpoises or something on it."

Pilot X laughed. "Well, I wasn't sure if you knew the distinction between a star and a planet. My apologies. Yes, it's a planet. And we believe, like you, it is mostly made of water.

But we believe it has air and land as well. You can see the dark shapes on it sometimes."

"Yeah, but they move," she said.

"Not all of them. There are lighter and darker ones. We think the lighter ones are immense clouds that bring rain. The darker ones are land. We think it is a world rich in plants and animals that could be a wonderful place to live."

"To live? You're cracked. How are we supposed to live in water?"

"Well, you wouldn't live on the water parts, just on the land."

"There's hardly any land, even if you are right about the dark parts! And if those are huge clouds, then it probably rains constantly. Sounds miserable. And what makes you think it has air?"

"You can see a penumbra on its edge."

"Humph." This point seemed to land with Lal. "That's interesting. I have noticed an aura. Hadn't ever thought about it meaning there was air. But OK. Let's say we get a lot of raincoats and decide we want to live on a wet, miserable rain planet. How would we ever get there?"

Pilot X sighed. "That's the trick, of course. One can imagine all kinds of ways, but they all have problems. Mostly how to get them off the ground." He could tell her, of course, but that would cross the line into interference.

"Gravity's a carnack's crotch, I always say. Plus, there may be air there, but I doubt it stretches all the way from here to there. We've sent up balloons. Things suffocate if they get too high. Just like climbing a mountain."

"You'd have to take air with you, I suppose," Pilot X hinted.

"HA! You're a loon. But I like you." She clinked her glass of garvee with him. It tasted like amber ale to Pilot X. It wasn't coffee, but it was quite good.

"So that's it? That's your great saying? Merva might be a good place to live if we ever figure out how to get there?" He could hear the smirk even if he couldn't really see her face. Pilot X had learned just enough about her so far to know that this meant she was entertaining the idea.

He leaned back and took a sip of garvee. "There's more to it, of course. But yes. We think there are places that are quite dry. Even some deserts. But most of all we think it solves the problem of food." This was another gamble. Verity deduced that food allocation, or at least consistent harvests, was a problem on the dying planet.

"What food problem?"

"Where I am from, our harvests are too variable. It becomes difficult to plan and store."

"Oh, that food problem. Yeah, a farmer issue. Not my concern. Not unless the garvee runs out."

"Well, it may become yours and everyone's concern if it gets worse."

"Maybe," Lal said with another sniff. "I admit, you have me curious. I'd like more details. But in any case, I can try to help you find your stuff. Let's drink on it." She poured some garvee from her bottle into the glass and Pilot X guessed he was expected to do the same. They clinked glasses again and drank. It was good beer.

"So, is garvee like your bire or however you said it?" she asked.

"Beer. And yes. Like a fine amber ale," he said.

"A bamboo sail? Whatever. It'll always be garvee to me. To the Wisdomer!"

PREPARATIONS

THAT EVENING, LAL took Pilot X to a telescope mounted away from the settlement so they could look at Merva and talk more about Pilot X's "research." He felt like it was his chance to clinch the deal. It was a long walk and Lal let Jorendren come too as long as he carried some food and, of course, garvee. Pilot X had made him get a gendran circle, too.

"You actually like that stuff? Too sweet for me," Lal said, but paid for it anyway. They reached a neighborhood where the houses were not right next to one another and were occasionally punctuated by fields. On the edge of a field of something that looked like corn sat a telescope pointed up at the sky.

"First the saying, then the eating," Lal grumbled, as if it were a rule she needed to follow and not her own plan. Pilot X spent some time pointing out the indications of Merva's atmosphere. He was able to find a few patches of brown that indicated there was dry land down there. They spent about a half hour observing and noting various details for Lal to investigate. Lal was still skeptical but didn't criticize.

"Well, it's something worth studying," she said. "Let's think about it over garvee. And some food."

Jorendren happily prepared a perfect picnic scene in a flat area by the road, away from the telescope. Pilot X thought it an odd location choice, but there wasn't much traffic on the road. Though he had seen a few steam-powered vehicles in Ladren, most people got around on foot or occasionally rode on a light gray animal that had the head of a sheep on an almost impossibly thin body with six legs, two of which sort of stuck out from the sides and hit the ground every so often. Pilot X couldn't tell if they helped adjust speed or stabilized the animal. And he hadn't quite caught the name of it. It sounded something like *throat*.

"Pily, I must say, you have my wheels turning. I wonder what other secrets may be hidden in the other planets. Think of Morbion or Janus? They're so much brighter. Maybe they're hot? Maybe they're young stars? What would that mean?" She chuckled to herself. "In any case, it's a great thing to get excited again at my age. To thinking!" she said, and raised her glass of garvee.

Pilot X drank to her toast. He went straight from that to the pie, causing a stern look from Jorendren for breaking protocol. But Lal didn't say anything, so it was fine. The meat was in a small bread bowl. It looked like chicken but tasted more like fish. Like a really meaty fish.

They talked about all kinds of things that Pilot X would call science, from physics to biology and even a little math. Pilot X wished Verity could be there. He didn't risk exposing his communication device again. He wondered if she was listening.

Eventually the conversation turned to the parts Pilot X was looking for. *Here we go*, he thought, and leaned forward to hear Lal better. The garvee had his ears ringing a little bit.

"I can ask around, but I think I would have heard if they were here. Devices like these would be the talk of the sayers,"

Lal said. "But I know someone who might know more. He's far away, but I could send word. His name is Prishat."

Pilot X noticed Jorendren shudder at the name.

"He lives way up north in Kindren," Lal continued. "Jorendren doesn't like him." She snickered but not with real humor. "Many don't. They sometimes say he's a dark sayer, because of how informed he is. Frankly, I don't know how he does it. But if anybody would know about your things, it would be old Prishat."

Pilot X didn't love chasing off after another unknown, but then this was the approach he had adopted. And who knows? Maybe this person was not from Vagson. Maybe he was like Pilot X and hiding out here, which is why these more primitive people were suspicious and so impressed by him. Which would make him much more likely to have the parts!

Also, this helped prove his approach to Verity. See? He had drifted into town and the universe had pointed him to the smartest person on the planet. Or at least to a person who liked beer who could point him to the smartest person on the planet. "I would be grateful for an introduction," Pilot X said.

"An introduction!" Lal almost spat out her garvee. "I'll send word and ask him. You don't need to travel all the way to Kindren yourself to find out!"

"How will you send word?" Pilot X asked.

"Pily." She fixed him with one steely eye. "Sometimes I think you're fooling us and you don't know nothing. Or you're just making fun of us locals. Ain't you ever heard of a Rider?"

Pilot X of course did not know what that meant here. He ventured a guess: "A courier?"

"What's a coo-rear?" Lal asked.

"A courier is someone who takes messages at a fast clip from place to place," Pilot X said.

Lal slapped the ground. "You mean someone who *rides* from place to place carrying messages? Like, oh, I don't know, say, a *Rider*?"

Pilot X laughed. "Well, yes. We call them couriers."

"Well, whatever for? Anyway, yes, I'll send a cootiebird up north with a message."

"How long will that take?"

"Oh, Riders can usually make it up there in less than eight days. Give him a couple days to decide to respond—should be around twenty days or less."

Pilot X could be in Kindren tomorrow, but he couldn't very well admit that.

"I could have my answer in eight days or twenty, is what you're saying?"

"Ha! Well, now look at you? In a hurry? I guess I would be too. I forgot you didn't come all this way to sit for a while in Ladren, wasting your time with an old sayer, Wisdomer bless you. Of course, you'll go. You're like me. Stiff-minded when you have a purpose. I respect that. All right. I'll give you directions and write you a letter of recommendation, too," she said.

"Thank you, Lal."

"You don't even mention it, Pily. To the Wisdomer!"

"To the Wisdomer."

STANDOFF

AS THEY WALKED, Lal was entertaining herself by making Jorendren tell stories that Pilot X could tell were meant to be embarrassing. He just didn't have the cultural literacy to understand most of the references. Except the one where Jorendren had lost the denim bits that made up his pants. That was embarrassing in any culture.

They were coming up a side street to one of the main thoroughfares that led back to Lal's house, when three silhouettes blocked the road.

"That you, Rel?" Lal said without any hint of concern. It was amazing that she thought she knew who it was since all Pilot X saw was a shadow. Did she have some kind of special night vision?

"Can smell him a mile away," Lal muttered.

Maybe special smelling powers?

They finally got close enough to see. It was the raggedy man and his two lanky friends.

"Your guest there," said the raggedy man. "He punched me."

"Pily, did you punch Rel?" Lal asked in a flat tone.

"Yeah, he tried to steal my—bracelet."

Lal said, "Humph. Rel, did you try to steal his—what the hell you wearing a bracelet for? Anyway, did you try to steal it, Rel?"

"We was making him pay the fee," said Rel, a bit peevish.

"Uh-huh." Lal sighed and scratched her nose. "Well, Pily. He's got a throat-manure reason, but you did punch him." She shook her head. "By our way, he gets to have an answer fight."

"What's an answer fight?" Pilot X said.

She looked up at him and he had that rare moment of seeing her eyes. "He gets to try to punch you back."

"What if I punch him again first?" Pilot X said.

Lal laughed and patted Pilot X on the side. "Then you're clean and done. But you won't surprise him, and this is Rel. I know him. He's a sad sack of rags, but he's hard to punch if he suspects it's coming. Come on, Jorendren." Lal began to leave.

"Wait, you're just going to leave me here to get beat up?" Pilot X said.

Lal stopped short and turned. "What do you take me for, Pily? I'm going to get help. Try not to break yours or anyone else's neck until I get back."

"But he's got three people!" Pilot X shouted.

Lal just waved her hand at him.

"You accusing me of cheating?" Rel said, cracking his knuckles. "You insulting me? Saying I won't hold to code?"

Pilot X didn't know what most of that meant.

"All right, let's get this over with," Pilot X said, holding up his hands like an ancient boxer. Lal was more right than she knew about the sucker punch. Pilot X knew next to nothing about proper fighting.

As he was holding his fists up and Rel was smiling and beginning to move toward him, he noticed a diagram on his communications device.

It showed a fair line drawing of Pilot X holding his hands in an odd way and kicking a short, squat, less-accurate representation of Rel. Pilot X could barely tell what the line version of him was supposed to do. He could not hope to execute that move without practice.

Rel was within arm's reach now and starting to dance. Pilot X made a brief move forward and Rel leaped back out of the way. He was light on his feet.

"So if I let you punch me, this is over?"

Rel laughed. "I can punch you as many times as I want and take your bracelet, too," he said. "*Then* it's over."

Pilot X sighed. Then he noticed something. On the side where Lal had just patted him, he felt something hard. Rel danced in and took a swing during the distraction. Pilot X stumbled backward and fell. Rel and his companions laughed. "This is a gendran circle," Rel said.

When he fell, Pilot X felt the hard thing dislodge. Somehow Lal had attached a thin rod of very hard wood to his side. The rod had a leather loop in one end that had some kind of sticky material that he guessed had latched it onto his clothing.

Pilot X grabbed the rod; just by holding it, he could tell it was dense.

Rel made to kick Pilot X, who tried to grab his foot but ended up letting the rod get kicked out of his hand into the dark by the side of the street. Rel didn't seem to notice.

Pilot X kept dancing back toward that side as Rel kept trying to swing. Pilot X now understood what people meant when they said someone had reach. Rel did not have the reach to get to Pilot X.

"Stand still, you coward!" shouted Rel, and ran at him, knocking him down with a bear hug.

They fell in the darkened side of the street and Pilot X felt blood trickle down his face. He also felt the rod. Rel released him to get up and get a better angle to punch Pilot X in the head.

Pilot X swung the rod at Rel's head and made contact. Rel dropped to the ground immediately and didn't get up. The lanky men stopped shouting encouragement and gasped. They ran over.

"You killed him," said one.

"No, he's breathing," said the other.

Pilot X backed away. It was probably the most violent thing he had ever done. He was shocked with himself.

After a minute, Lal returned with a woman dressed all in red.

"Oh," she said when she saw Pilot X standing. "You found it. Wasn't sure you'd catch on." She pointed at the unconscious Rel and turned to the woman in red. "Looks like he got sapped with a drury rod." The woman in red winced. "I'll let you take care of it."

"Come on, Pily. Before his friends get over their grief. Besides, we need to get you a place to stay."

"Oh, I have a place outside of town."

"Well, fine, Mr. Mystery. Then we at least have to have another garvee in honor of your victory before you go."

"I could use one. It'd help my aching head."

"Good for what ails you!" shouted Lal.

NORTH

KINDREN WAS HIGH up on the far edge of the farthest northern inhabited continent. The air was thin there and the ground was mostly frozen. Verity recommended oxygen canisters, but Pilot X ruled it out as too conspicuous, since Verity's observations didn't indicate any of the locals used them. He settled for a shot of oxygen-concentration enhancer.

Verity landed far from the settlement, since there wasn't much vegetation to hide in. That meant a long walk for Pilot X. He argued with her about what to wear and eventually put on a huge furry thing.

"Are you sure you don't want a thicker coat?" she asked.

"If I had a thicker coat, I'd have to roll into town."

"I just don't want you to get chilled on your walk and arrive ill."

"I'm more worried about getting answers from this Prishat person. Wait, are you worrying about me?"

"I am not worrying; I am making rational observations and extrapolating helpful advice."

"I'm glad you care. I'll be fine."

"You should take a weapon."

"A weapon? Since when do I take weapons?"

"You could have used one in your fight."

This was the first time she had mentioned the fight with Rel. "It's not likely Rel followed me here."

"The chances of Rel following you here are low but not impossible, since we traveled enough time in the future to make it plausible you traveled here by thgroaght." Pilot X wondered how Verity had learned to pronounce the name of the six-legged animal. There was no database on this planet to tap into.

"Rel didn't follow me. He's in whatever passes for a hospital here. I don't need a gun."

"What about a dart gun?"

Pilot X rolled his eyes. He really wanted to get going.

"Fine. A dart gun." He marched into the singularity chamber and found a dart gun lying under an old spear and a few other primitive weapons.

He returned to the cockpit, held up the dart gun, and then shoved it away into the folds of his thick coat.

"Good. I will monitor your vitals and message you if I notice anything that requires you to return. Please authorize auto-engage for retrieval in case you are unable to return on your own."

"Is that really necessary?"

"Please authorize auto—"

"Fine, but only if I'm nonresponsive *and* my vitals are ninety percent off baseline."

"Fifty percent."

"It's not an auction."

"Sixty percent."

"OK, fine. Sixty percent."

"Have a safe walk into town." Verity sounded cheery.

The walk was uneventful, and the town of Kindren was empty. Verity had observed that, of the eight thousand people who lived in Kindren, only a few usually moved around, mostly in the middle of the day. Pilot X assumed it was because of the cold. There didn't seem to be a market or a pattern of commuting. From what Verity could guess, people worked where they lived and only left their houses to do tasks or make supply purchases at a handful of warehouses. They could not determine what Kindren's major industry was either. There were no factories and no docks. What fishing and hunting was done seemed to be done by small groups and mostly for personal use with limited local trade.

Lal gave Pilot X the name of the only hotel in Kindren. She'd said, "You'll find it easy enough if you can ask someone, but sometimes it's hard to find somebody to ask. And they don't use signs in that flat ice patch of a town."

Pilot X had no way to pay for a room anyway, so he skipped the hotel and headed straight for Prishat's house. He had come to this planet for answers and Prishat might be his only chance. If they came up empty here, they'd have to go back to Parthian Prime, and he very much did not want to go back to Parthian Prime. The thought of the Matriarch made him shudder. He wanted nothing to do with her, but he wasn't sure he could trust himself to withstand a second round of flirting. He had been too distracted and distrustful for it to work the first time around. He worried he might be too weak and lonely to resist a second round, and he was certain he and his memory of Alexandra could not live with that. So Prishat better have the answers.

Because they didn't have street signs in Kindren, Pilot X had memorized the directions. Off the main road he had to take the third right and then the second left. Among the endless rows of unmarked low black structures, he found the row Lal had described as having a huge, bell-shaped iron cage at the end. And by huge, Lal had meant huge. It was big enough to hold Verity with room to spare. But there was nothing in it. Pilot X had no idea what it had been for and Lal hadn't explained.

The fourth house down the row was suppoed to have the vents of a steam shop on it. That would be Prishat's house. It wasn't a steam shop, just his house, but he carried on some steam experiments there and did a little trade with people based on it.

He found the house, though no steam was coming out of the vents. He walked up and knocked at the door. He heard nothing, and nobody came. He waited a bit and knocked again. Still nothing. No sounds came from the house.

"He's gone for fish," someone said. Pilot X turned and saw a very tall, very red-haired woman wrapped in very purple furs standing outside the front door of the house next door.

"For fish, you say?" Pilot X answered.

"Yeah. Won't be back for a bit. You're welcome to wait in here if you like. Name's Mindhar."

"Pilot X," he said.

"What?" She looked confused.

"My name is Pilot X."

"Well, your mean momma." She laughed. "Still, it's as good a name as any. Come in if you like. I've got tea on. Or not, as you please. Just being neighborly." She turned to go back into her house. Pilot X normally wouldn't follow a strange lady into a strange house in a strange frozen city on a strange planet. But he was impatient for answers, had an AI-driven timeship available on demand, and he doubted the lady was associated with Rel or the people who had tried to steal Verity. Besides, he needed somewhere warm to wait for Prishat. And small-town people were more trustworthy, right? Plus, she might have pie. He decided to risk it. Her door had just closed by the time he got there, but he opened it and went on in, and she didn't seem to mind.

Inside was one big room with dark wooden walls. In a corner opposite the front door was a collection of things that Pilot X guessed served as a kitchen. She was over there, presumably getting the tea. "Have a seat," she said over her shoulder. "Anywhere's fine."

There was a long, backless cushiony thing, but Pilot X felt like he wanted a back to rest against, so he chose one of the four steel chairs with padded white seats near a table.

"Hungry?" she asked without looking.

"A bit. I've been on the road," he added. He didn't want to put this stranger out, but if she had what he hoped she had . . .

"I have a Kindren circle that will knock your socks off," she said, and reached up into a cabinet and pulled out a very large pie. If she hadn't lived in such a horrible land and if he wasn't prevented from interfering in this planet's history, he might have found himself a bit in love with Mindhar just then.

She brought over two cups of an unremarkable hot brown liquid that was not coffee and didn't even smell like tea. Most importantly, she brought two slices of what looked like a delectable berry pie. The smooth round berries were ridiculously dark. Light could not escape these berries.

"You ever have Kindren berries before?" she asked, noticing his look.

"I can't say I have."

"Well, they grow everywhere here, so we get used to them. I think they're tasty enough, but outsiders seem to fall in love with them. It's our principal export. Keeps the town running, actually. Everybody puts in some mandatory berry-picking time. Once a year, the city office manages the harvest collection and export and we all get a check. Lets us do whatever we want. A lot of artists and sayers up here."

Well, that explained that. "What do you do besides let perfect strangers from far-off lands into your house and serve them p—berry circles?"

"Ha. Manual labor mostly. We don't get many visitors here and nobody would travel all this way in all this cold to do us much harm. We don't have much to take and even less to lose. It makes it easy for us to be friendly if we want to be. Mind you, not everybody thinks like me. And I came here to think. I do a bit of philosophy. Nobody ever liked my thoughts much in the philosophical collectives, so I just said forget them and moved here to think and pick berries and build fences and relax. And serve Kindren berry circles to strangers from far-off lands." She laughed again. Pilot X found it musical. "It's a little cold, but other than that I can't complain. What brings you to visit Prishat, if you can say?"

"Lal recommended I visit him."

"Don't know Lal. Another sayer, like him?"

"Yeah. Lives in Ladren."

"Oh wait. Covers her face and feet along with everything else?"

"That's her."

"Didn't recall her name. Or maybe never knew it. Met her a couple times, though."

She didn't ask a follow-up question, but Pilot X figured he was here to find things and he wouldn't find them by keeping it a secret. "I come from Alenda. It's very far away." Mindhar shook her head to indicate she didn't know it. It was convenient being on a planet where people knew other lands existed on the planet but not what those lands were called or where they were.

"We had some saying devices—I guess that's what you call them—that were taken from us and we're trying to track them down. Lal said Prishat is most likely to know if anybody has talked about them."

"She's not wrong. How that man knows what he does, I cannot tell you. He's in the most remote town in existence that gets the fewest Riders ever, and he knows everything happening on half the continent."

If Pilot X was right, this might be the wrong guy to use the name Alenda around. He'd barely gotten away with it with the Matriarch because she knew the name from a fairy tale and thought he was joking. Here it would give him away as someone from off planet to someone else who might also be from off planet.

Mindhar cocked her head. "Speak of the Wisdomer and he shall grant you wishes. I think I heard his door."

GUESSES

PRISHAT HAD WHITE hair everywhere but his head. A white beard, white eyebrows, white ear hair, and even white bushy hair on his hands. His head, though, was a smooth, wrinkle-free dome. He wore something like glasses, though they only covered the outside half of each of his eyes.

Mindhar motioned toward Pilot X. "Prishat, this is Piludex. Friend of Lal's down in Ladren. She sent him here to talk to you."

Prishat just stared out the doorway.

"Well, I'll leave you to it then." Mindhar headed to her house without a look back.

"I have fish," Prishat said, turning away from the door but leaving it open. Pilot X took it as an invitation.

As dark and spare as Mindhar's house had been, Prishat's was darker and sparer. He had a cot and one old wooden chair. His food-prep area was half as full as Mindhar's. One cabinet sat on the countertop, leaning precariously against the wall. Plaster peeked out between vast paper maps that covered the other walls. Pilot X couldn't make any sense of the maps. They were made up of a lot of lines. Charts, maybe?

"Nice charts," Pilot X ventured.

Prishat merely continued to drop fish into a container that looked like some kind of cooler. Pilot X busied himself trying to figure out what the charts were. One looked like it noted orbital velocities. It had the right number of lines to be charting the system's planets.

"You know, I was telling Lal about some information regarding Merva."

"The water. Life support," he said.

"How do you know? I just told her before I left for here." He didn't mention that he'd left for here at what was this morning (for him) in his timeship but eight days ago (in real time).

Prishat looked right at him. "You're not from here."

"No, I'm not."

"No, I mean not from this planet."

"I—" Pilot X's blood ran cold.

"Doesn't matter. I won't tell anyone. They wouldn't believe me anyway. But since you know about things I probably couldn't understand, I'll go ahead and tell you how I know things. It'll seem like child's play to you, I expect."

Pilot X listened carefully for a trap, while letting himself hope the slightest bit that Prishat might in fact know who had ordered the parts of the Instant.

"But you can't tell Lal. Or anyone else who's a sayer," Prishat continued.

"I promise."

"I can hear really well." Prishat broke out in a smile and began laughing maniacally.

"That's—that's funny." Pilot X's heart sank. The man was just insane. And maybe a lucky guesser.

"It is!" Prishat shouted. "Have a seat, Pilot X." He'd pronounced the name perfectly.

"You won't tell me your secret."

"No, no, I will. Sort of." He sat down himself and sighed. "I deduce. I observe and deduce and collect. I use my mind, that's all. Everything I know is mostly right in front of everyone else. You're wondering how I pronounced your name right when Mindhar and Lal got it wrong. I listened to the way you said things. Your accent. I derived what I know about how Mindhar talks to reverse engineer it from the way you talk. Got pretty close, too, didn't I?"

"Dead accurate."

"And you went straight for my map of orbital velocities. Two, maybe three, other people on this planet would recognize what those are. Add a few other details you dropped to the fact that I know what impresses Lal and what she does at her favorite picnic spot. That led me to guess about Merva. It's more complicated than that, but that's the gist."

"What's my ship's name?"

This one caught Prishat off guard. "Ship? Oh! Ship of the sky! Right?"

"Exactly," he said. And Pilot X saw the limit of Prishat's and the planet's understanding in that one statement. It left him little hope, but he had to try anyway. "Look, I'll save you some time, since you can deduce most of it. I'm looking for machines. They were stolen. Well, that's a lie and you'll know it. They were created on another planet and I was told they were delivered here. But it doesn't make sense, because they couldn't possibly be used by anyone I've seen here. And you're the only person I've met who even knows people from other planets exist."

"What machines?" Prishat asked.

"Damn," Pilot X said. He showed the papers to Prishat.

"I've neither heard of nor deduced anything like them. I don't know what to tell you about that. If I were to lay odds, I'd say they were never here and you were lied to. But if that's not the case, my next best guess is that someone hid them in Heraclor. It's the most manufacture-oriented of the known countries. They wouldn't stick out much there if someone weren't looking closely. And it's far from here, which might keep any details from me. It's a long journey. Months or maybe more than a year. Why don't you stay awhile? I could gather so much good detail from you. It would be very helpful. And I can tell Mindhar likes you. I'm sure you'd enjoy yourself."

Pilot X was distraught. For a moment the thought of returning to the Matriarch drove him to seriously consider giving up the search and settling down with Mindhar. But he couldn't. Even though Alexandra was nonexistent, he wouldn't let himself do that to her. Even though she would never know. His dreams of her lately were so real, he didn't want to face her even there. No, he wouldn't give up on Vagson. Not yet.

Pilot X thanked Prishat. Before he could leave, Mindhar stopped by again and invited them both for dinner. He craved company, so he let himself forget everything and enjoy the food and conversation. It was limited conversation. Much of it about fish. But it was exactly what Pilot X needed to clear his head and avoid the sinking stone of disappointment he felt in his gut. He even stayed the night at Mindhar's. On the floor.

The next morning Prishat came over with a fish and Mindhar fried it up and served it with hard bread for breakfast. Apparently, this was a fancy version of Kindren breakfast.

"We usually just eat boiled grain," Prishat said. After saying his good-byes and leaving Prishat with some excellent details about all manner of things he didn't think would advance technology too much, Pilot X began the long trudge out of town.

He was halfway back to Verity when a hump in the road stood up and yelled at him. It was Rel.

"There's no one to help you now, outlander. I know what you are!"

Pilot X sighed. He should call Verity and have her land on him. "What do you want, Rel? We're even. How did you even get here?"

"I rode a thgroaght till it died, then rode another and kept on. I will end you, wizard outlander."

Pilot X scowled. "What do you mean, *wizard*?"

"I saw you leave your little house. A house that wasn't built there. I saw you talking to someone who wasn't there. You're evil."

Well, that settled it. Pilot X was tired and Rel could not be trusted with this information. Pilot X pulled out the dart gun.

Rel laughed. "I won't let you near enough to hit me again."

Pilot X shot Rel. He collapsed in a heap.

"Best of luck Rel," he said.

VISIT

SOMEONE KNOCKED ON Lal's door. That would be Jorendren. "You better have that gear grease I told you not to forget," she said, not caring if he could hear her through the door or not. "And why don't you think to add a couple of bottles of garvee on your own?" she added, then stopped as she opened the door.

It wasn't Jorendren. A tall, muscular woman with pink hair stood in front of a lump of a man in a white shirt and blue pants. "May we come in?" the woman said with a smirk, not waiting for Lal to say "yes" or minding that she almost knocked Lal down as she pushed past.

The lumpy man muttered a "sorry" as he squeezed past as well.

"Who the frolicking molly are you?" Lal said at the same time as Prellix demanded, "Where is he?"

"Where's who?" Lal sneered. "Get out of my house."

"The alien? The ship's pilot. You know who I mean?" Prellix spat. "We'll leave as soon as you tell me where he is." Prellix said this while pacing menacingly through Lal's room, picking up anything that looked like it might be fragile.

"I don't know who you mean, and you better stop touching things you don't understand and get out of here. I'm calling the watch." Lal made for the door.

"Paul," Prellix commanded.

The lumpy Paul had been standing quietly by the door since they'd come in, and now moved to block it. "Sorry," he said. "You just need to tell us where the—man—is and she'll let us go."

"Us?" Lal laughed. "This one doesn't seem much help, pinky?" She pointed at Paul then made for the door again, but Paul stood his ground.

"Please. Just tell her what she wants," Paul pleaded.

"Maybe if she leaves and comes back and asks nicely," Lal said. Then she tried to push Paul out of the way.

"Lady!" Paul said, frustrated as they struggled. "This is really unnecessary." Lal was trying everything to get past, and she had almost slipped away.

"You'd better not let her go, Paul!" Prellix threatened.

"You said no names!" Paul said, even though this was the second time Prellix had called him Paul out loud. Lal took the opportunity of his distraction to duck under his arm.

"Get her or I get you!" Prellix yelled.

Paul made a noise like an angry child, then turned and grabbed Lal by the cloth around her neck before she could get downstairs, throwing her back into the room. She landed with a thud at Prellix's feet.

"Now," Prellix said, holding a particularly fragile-looking glass item and dangling it as if to drop it. "You tell me what I want to know—"

But Lal wasn't moving. Her green eyes stared up at Prellix through the towels around her face. Her neck was at a very improbable angle.

"Damn it, Paul," Prellix said, and knelt down, digging through the cloth to find a pulse. After a moment she said, "I'm pretty sure she's dead."

Paul's eyes widened.

"Do you know what you've done?" Prellix said.

Paul hit himself in the head. "I killed the person before they could tell us what we wanted to know," he said, and kept hitting himself. "Stupid, Stupid. Stupid."

Prellix nodded. "Again. And what did I say?"

"No dinner when I preacherly kill someone," he said, stopping the self-punishment.

"Prematurely, not preacherly. But yes."

"I'm sorry, sis."

"Tell that to your empty stomach tonight."

They left Lal's apartment. Neither one of them looked back.

SEARCHING

"VERITY, WE NEED to get some medical help for Rel. Is there some way we can—they don't have phones, do they?"

"Rel is dead," Verity said.

"What?"

"I monitored your shot. He died of heart failure shortly after you left."

"No. I—I didn't want to kill—"

"I'm sorry. There was nothing you could have done. He must have had a weak heart."

Pilot X hated himself for feeling relief that Rel wouldn't be able to contaminate the development of Vagson now.

"Prishat didn't know anything," Pilot X said, changing the subject. He slumped into his chair and shut off any feelings about Rel, complex or otherwise. He couldn't add more guilt. It would be the feather that broke the thgroaght's back.

Verity answered, "I suppose we will need to develop an excuse to return to Parthian Prime then—"

"No," Pilot X said, and began punching in coordinates.

"My navigation is partially down for maintenance," Verity said.

Pilot X stopped. "No, it's not," he said without looking up from punching in the numbers.

"It will be down for an unspecified amount of time," said Verity.

"Just stop—"

"Planetary navigation is functional," she said.

"I said—"

"Is there somewhere on the planet you'd like to go?"

Pilot X finally stopped trying to punch in coordinates to the planet with his hut and looked up. "You were eavesdropping," he whispered.

"I believe Heraclor is a location that might be useful to investigate," she prodded.

Pilot X shook his head. He didn't want to admit she was right. But she wasn't even giving him a chance to argue. He started to yell, but the rock in his gut weighed too much. "Fine," he said.

"You want to go to Heraclor?" Verity asked.

"Now you're just getting pushy."

"We could just wait here for systems to come back online and then return to the Matriarch."

Pilot X laughed. He wasn't sure if Verity was being mean or telling a joke, but of course Verity was an AI. He liked to pretend like she was developing a sense of humor, but could she really? He doubted it. Which meant she really was just proposing options. And she really had off-planet navigational difficulties. It wasn't impossible. Bugs showed up occasionally and she'd gone a long time without proper maintenance.

He muttered, "Prishat said maybe Heraclor. There's a lot of manufacturing there." Just saying the words out loud gave him momentum, the way hearing the name of the Matriarch gave him motivation. "And if that doesn't work"—he sighed, gathering his strength—"we keep looking." His voice got stronger and he sat up. "Plot out a course to visit areas likely to harbor the parts of the Instant in descending order of probability."

"An excellent plan," Verity said.

He swore he could hear a smirk. Maybe he was wrong about Verity after all. If he was, he realized he was probably very wrong.

Heraclor was similar to Ladren but with more and larger steam shops. He found people who understood the machine diagrams slightly better than Lal, but they still didn't know what they really were and certainly had never heard of them. Heraclorians, though, were one of the few people who knew of the Galdians, who were on the other side of the planet. The sea-loving Galdians pointed him to the island people of Brilan, who in turn introduced him to the southern polar race of the Celor, a sort of Kindren on the other end of the planet. He repeated the process until he had a comprehensive political geography of Vagson and had visited almost every nation on it. In each place, he directed the local scientific attention to the other inhabitable planet in the stellar system, hoping to plant seeds that would help the people of Vagson save themselves someday. Each place he visited had a local version of pie. No place had anyone who knew anything useful about the parts of the Instant.

"Well, Verity. As suspected, we were lied to," said Pilot X at a sink in the singularity chamber, trying to rinse the taste of jarga fruit out of his mouth after he had eaten one of the least pleasant versions of pie ever in the Yellick Basin. "And I'd say we've done more than our due diligence on that point." He spat.

"There is a thirty-two-percent chance that the Matriarch of Parthian Prime intentionally lied to you. There is now a seventy-four-percent chance that she was lied to by someone, possibly Steiv, without her knowledge."

"Any guesses why anyone would send me off on this wild-goose chase?"

"It is most likely that someone saw you as a threat to Parthian Prime and decided to get you out. There is a smaller possibility that the thieves who wanted to steal me were able to concoct the plan. The least likely possibility is that the originators of this new version of the Instant discovered you were after them."

"No percentages?"

"The percentages are—"

"Never mind. We should go."

"Go where?" Verity said.

He almost said *home*, but that wasn't right. He didn't have a home. Only a hut. He started to feel the old despair creeping in again. He fought it back. eHeHHH "Parthian Prime," he said, with more confidence than he felt. He would steel himself to face the Matriarch. "Tell them the info didn't pan out, and try to get the Matriarch to give me better intel."

"That seems to be the only option," said Verity.

"And we need more coffee. I have all this pie, after all." Pilot X had started stashing away an extra pie in every location he visited. He had several refrigerators full of pie in the singularity storage chamber. None of them were jarga fruit. "But let's go say good-bye to Lal first. I want to thank her."

GONE

PILOT X SKIPPED up the creaking, unstable steps to Lal's room above the steam shop and knocked on the door. Jorendren answered.

"Oh, Jorendren. Hello. Good to see you. Is Lal home?"

"No." Jorendren's head sagged.

"What's wrong?" Pilot X said, noticing the distinct lack of words from the usually verbose and cheery Jorendren.

"She's . . ."

"What?" Pilot X was concerned. "She's what, Jorendren?"

"Dead," said a voice behind him. It was a man dressed all in white, wearing gloves. "Did you know Lal?" he asked.

"Well, yes," said Pilot X. "I just visited her—well—I guess it would have been late last year for you," he said. "What happened?"

"I am Gareveld. I am only the Finalizer. It is not for me to say." He nodded to Jorendren, as if to say Pilot X should ask him. Jorendren looked at a loss.

"Jorendren, let me get you something to drink or eat maybe?" Pilot X said.

"Garvee," was all Jorendren said, and led the way.

They got two bottles of Garvee and sat on a bench in what Pilot X assumed was some kind of café, although it looked more like an open marketplace inside a thgroaght barn.

"This used to be a thgroaght barn," Jorendren said. "Lal introduced me to it. 'One of the new innovations,' she called it. A new way of selling . . ." He just stared at his bottle.

"I'm so sorry, Jorendren. If you don't want to talk about it, I understand. Did she get ill?"

"Murdered," Jorendren said.

"What?"

"Killed. That's what the watch determined. Attempted burglary. But they didn't take anything. Must have got scared. Didn't mean to kill her, they said. But they did." He was crying softly now.

"Why would someone kill Lal? Why would anyone even try to steal from Lal?"

Jorendren just shook his head. "Strangers. Some people in the steam shop saw them go up. Heard some noises and then saw them leave."

"Strangers?" Pilot X asked.

"Yeah, a giant woman with pink hair and a fat man," said Jorendren. "That's what they said, anyway. I never saw them. Just found her when I got back with the gear grease like she asked. I didn't forget. But now she'll never know. She was just lying there all bent. Oh, Lal," he sobbed into his garvee.

Pilot X's wrist buzzed. Verity had sent him a picture of the two people who had tried to steal her back on Parthian Prime, a tall woman with pink hair and a fat man. Pilot X decided to risk showing it to Jorendren.

"Like this?" He showed him his wrist.

"Maybe," said Jorendren. "Could be. I never saw them."

Pilot X changed the subject to calm Jorendren down while they finished their garvee. But inside, his own rage was growing. To kill a defenseless old woman because they wanted to find him? That was unthinkable. But it had to be them.

Jorendren agreed to take Pilot X to the man at the steam shop who had seen the strangers. His name was Hordren.

"What is that thing? Never seen anything like that before," Hordren said when Pilot X showed him his wrist device. "And it shows you photographs right on it. Splendid."

"Bit of trickery," Pilot X said. "Not as impressive as it looks. I just keep the picture clipped under the glass." Hordren looked disappointed.

"Does it look like them?" Pilot X said, hoping to distract him.

"Yeah. Don't know how you captured the likeness so well, but yes. That's her. And that dumpy one I didn't get a good look at, but it could easily be the same one."

"Thank you," Pilot X said, tamping down his anger for a little longer.

After they left, Pilot X took Jorendren aside. "I need to go, but I want you to know, I'm so very sorry about what happened to Lal. And if I find these people someday—and I have a feeling I will—they will pay for what they did to Lal. I promise."

Jorendren looked sad but appreciative of Pilot X's words. "Thank you. I believe you would. But it wouldn't bring her back." He bowed his head and teared up again.

"Is there anything I can do for you before I go?"

Jorendren shook his head. "Just remember her," he said. "Remember how she was." And Jorendren unexpectedly hugged Pilot X. "She liked you. She didn't like hardly anyone, but she liked you. I hope you treasure that gift."

"I will." Pilot X found himself tearing up now.

ATTACK

"IT WAS THEM!" Pilot X ranted. "I don't know why they would do that, but they did. And, Verity, they will try to get you again, I know it, and when they do, we need to punish them. Murder!"

"Yes, we shall apprehend them and deliver them to the Vagson authorities."

"That is very—Verity—of you to say. And yes, I know it's right." He got a little more control of his anger thanks to Verity's words. And he had to keep it under control. This was something he couldn't fix, but at least he could help. And hopefully Lal had spread the word about Merva. He'd check in on them again later a few hundred years down the road in their history. But that could wait. For now, he had to go shake down a matriarch. And his anger at Lal's murder and the Matriarch's likely involvement with the thieves had him eager to do so.

"Let's get to Parthian Prime then. I have some questions," Pilot X said. He was not worried at all about succumbing to the Matriarch's feeble and transparent flirting anymore.

Verity made orbit around Vagson and had begun plotting a system exit route to take them back to Parthian Prime when she shook. She never shook when not actually flying somewhere actively.

"What was that?" But before Pilot X had finished the question, the red tactical lights came on and Verity switched the console to evasive-maneuvers interface.

"We are being attacked," she said.

"Who's attacking us and why? We're not a battleship. We don't even have guns!"

"Unknown. Hold on." Pilot X felt a judder and the attacking ship appeared on his console screen. It was a small but sleek fighter of some kind in the shape of a triangle. It was pitted and stained but it had guns. Pilot X watched as the ship began to fire upon an earlier version of Verity.

"Verity, what did you do?"

"It's a marginal paradox that will dissipate as long as we . . . there. It's fine." The *Verity* being fired on disappeared.

"That was risky. Are you sure your safety parameters are correct?"

"They're fine. Brace yourself."

Too late, Pilot X saw what Verity was doing. "Hey! Wait! I'm the pilot here. Stop flying autonomously—" But the rest of his sentence was lost in the crash. Verity had rammed the attacking ship.

"What are you doing? Just jump!"

"Jumping would take too long and give them an opportunity to fire and disable us. Ramming is the only option to disable them and avoid pursuit. Our materials' makeup is much stronger than theirs. Also, I have identified the heat signatures of the inhabitants of the attacking ship as Prellix and Paul, the two thieves who tried to steal me. Coming about for another jump and ram."

"Belay!" Pilot X yelled. Verity stopped. "Are you mad?" he shouted.

"I'm incapable of anger."

"I meant crazy, but actually, *angry* makes sense too. You're angry they tried to steal you!"

"I am taking advanced protective measures for a known threat. I have disabled their weapons in the maneuver. They are coming about. My second maneuver would have prevented that."

"And now you're sulky."

"I am incapable of sulking. Impact in five—"

"Oh crap. We should—"

"Too late," Verity said, and the thieves' ship crashed into the **Verity** this time.

In the course of the maneuvers, the two ships had left Vagson's orbit and were now caught in the water planet Merva's gravity.

"Let's bring you around for another pass on our terms this time," Pilot X barked.

"Unable to comply. We are in a gravity-well degradation burn. All tactical systems devoted to crash control now."

"What?"

"We're falling out of the sky on Merva."

"We're going to crash? We don't crash!"

"We're going to crash. I wish you hadn't belayed my maneuver."

"Regret?! This is turning into an encyclopedic day for your emergent emotions!" Pilot X yelled above the noise of the atmosphere trying to burn its way into Verity from the outside. There was a loud bang and a high-pitched whining of inertial counteractive measures. Pilot X felt his stomach fly up to his mouth. He wondered idly if his stone of disappointment might fly out with it. Instead, some garvee did.

The crash happened faster than he would have expected. He had never crashed in the *Verity* before. It was just one loud bang, a moment of vomit, and he was back in his chair like nothing had happened. A few loose objects, like pens and the pages of parts schematics, were scattered everywhere. But things were stunningly normal otherwise. Thank goodness for safety belts.

"We're OK!" he cheered.

Verity did not respond.

"Verity? Status!"

A metallic voice that was not Verity's said, "Main AI program offline in safety mode. Will reboot in estimated time not available. All controls manual. Ship status is grounded. Unknown repairs needed."

Crap. That wasn't good. "Verity—Ship—what's the ground observation?"

The metallic voice continued. "Enemy ship within one hundred clicks. Two thermal signs detected. Shall we engage?"

Sure, thought Pilot X. Good old Alendan template ops. It had a basic algorithm subsystem for ship's defenses but no actual ship's defenses. His was a timeship, essentially a glorified shuttle, not a battleship. He was tempted to go ahead and tell the subsystem to fire away, but he was afraid that would break it, and he needed it to run the ship until Verity's self-repair was finished. If she could repair herself, that is. He almost asked Verity about the probability of that and then realized she couldn't answer him. His euphoria at surviving was fast converting to blind panic. He needed air.

"No. I'm headed out. Alert me when Verity—when the AI is back online."

"Acknowledged."

They had crash-landed in a swamp. The ground was sopping wet, covered in a cold fog and filled with the sound of insects.

Pilot X looked back at Verity. Except, was it Verity if she wasn't in there? Was she in there? If she was offline, where did she go? He got ahold of himself and his pilot training kicked in. *Assess the situation.* There was some smoke coming out of her and some external damage too. It looked superficial, but he couldn't be sure. He would have to get her back online, see if she was spaceworthy, and get her somewhere he could do repairs.

And where was that? Since he had destroyed his universe, she had done her own maintenance. This is why he hadn't wanted to leave his hut. It was dangerous out here and there was no Alendan civilization making replacement parts anymore. No more Moon of Pantoon full of timeship repair stations under Alendan treaty. Even the Fringe Cascade would be no help. He needed Verity to invent a genius way to fix herself, except Verity would have to be online to do that, and without the genius fix she might not come back online. And the whole reason she was possibly dead was that he, in his arrogance, had decided to try to save the universe again.

"Idiot!" he yelled, and slapped himself in the face. "You didn't have a choice last time. This time you did. And you chose wrong, look! You chose wrong!" Tears streaked his face as he pointed at the broken ship.

"No," he said, and pursed his lips, now arguing with himself. "No, this wasn't my choice. This was their choice! Some jerks decided they wanted to steal you and instead they damaged you beyond repair, *after* killing my friend. *They* are the idiots. Damn them!"

Pilot X ran off into the swamp. He got a few yards before realizing he needed to be armed with more than just his anger. He ran back inside the ship, and ten minutes later he came out with the dart gun, a spear, and a bow and arrow that had been handmade by people no longer in existence.

"The Alendan parliament has officially declared war!" Pilot X shouted, then jumped away from himself and said, "You can't," then jumped back, continuing to have a conversation with himself.

"Why not?"

"The rule against unprovoked aggression." He was taking the part of the absent Verity.

"The—you mean Article Five of the Primary Conventions? The First Phase Renderings of the Guardians of Alenda?"

"Yes."

"Doesn't apply."

"I don't see how it doesn't apply." He was starting to imitate Verity's voice a little.

"I've been provoked!" He smiled.

"Attempted thievery does not meet the standard of war," he said in a fair imitation of Verity.

"There's another reason though." His smile got a little manic.

"What's the other reason?" His imitation of Verity faltered a bit.

"Because I said so." He smiled a manic, frightening smile.

"Your saying so doesn't change the rule." It was the best Verity imitation he had ever done.

"Doesn't it?"

"It doesn't."

"But I'm the last of the Alendans," he cackled now. "I'm all of the Alendans. I'm the entire Alendan military."

"But the rule remains and only the Guardians of Alenda in parliament can amend the articles of any Phase of the Renderings. I am a robot. I have no feelings. *Bleep Blop. Blorp.*" His Verity imitation fell apart at the end.

Pilot X laughed maniacally through every word of his response to himself. "I was recently elected as parliament.

Fantastic! Now, as the only officer, I declare parliament in session. Your Honor? Yes, the Chair recognizes Pilot X. Thank you, me. It is with great humbleness and largesse of pomposity and overwrought prose that I put before you a proposed declaration of war with the plain facts that our entire civilization—including our entire AI cohort and, may I say, potentially every other civilization—has been put in peril by the actions of these thieves. What say you, Chair?"

"Voice vote." It was no longer Verity but some generic Alendan official he imitated now. "Say aye for war. Aye!"

He jumped again fast and said "aye" again.

He jumped one last time and in his fake official voice said, "Let the record show unanimity in support of the declaration of war." His imitation shifted to that of a military general. "The commander in chief orders you to mobilize and clear the area of enemies. Advance!"

Pilot X marched off into the swamp, his anger no longer erratic but instead boiling at a deadly level of sustained outrage.

Verity did not respond.

THE GUN

PRELLIX AND PAUL crawled out of their ship. It was a banged-up mess, but at least Prellix had brought it in for a controlled landing, not a crash. Paul admired her skill. It wasn't flyable at the moment, but she had told Paul it was reparable. Paul was limping and Prellix had a nasty cut on her forehead, but otherwise they were both in one piece. They heard the pilot of the other ship talking loudly off in the distance.

"How many are with him?" Paul asked.

"I can't tell." Prellix was helping Paul walk. "Sit down over here." Prellix pointed to a patch of relatively dry dirt that rose up out of the wet ground. Paul gingerly lowered himself to the ground, his leg stuck out in front of him bent at the knee, unable to bend under him in a more comfortable position.

They could still hear the other man shouting.

"Well, at least we know where his ship is," Prellix said. "Look, Paul, you're in no condition to come with me, but I'm going to go. They won't know it's just me, and I can hide in the trees so he won't get a fix on me. Besides, he won't expect anything. From the sound of it, he doesn't know we're here. You just hang out and I'll be back."

"Wait!" Paul yelled before she could get too far.

"Shhh," she said. "You're blowing my advantage. What is it?" she finished in a loud whisper.

"Where's the other gun?" He pointed at the handgun Prellix had drawn.

"There is no other gun," she said.

"Well, what should I use then?"

"For what?"

"To defend myself," Paul said.

"Your wit," Prellix snapped, and moved off.

The man's shouting reached a crescendo and Paul heard movement. He expected to hear a shot and then Prellix's voice calling him, but he didn't. Instead he just heard rustling. It could have been a pig or a bird for all he could tell. He thought maybe it sounded more violent than that, but he wasn't sure if it was his imagination.

He heard a whooshing sound that he couldn't identify and a thwack of something getting hit. He hoped it wasn't Prellix. He heard the whooshing sound again, but this time it was followed by more of a thunk and a groan, though he couldn't tell who had made the groan. He didn't know if he had ever heard Prellix groan and he certainly hadn't heard the other man groan, since he'd never even met him.

The rustling continued, which meant whoever had groaned was probably still on their feet. Some more whacks and odd whooshes followed, and Paul heard more grunts and groans from two different voices, but it gave him no clue of who, if anyone, had the upper hand.

"OK, troop!" a man yelled. "Flanking maneuver. Cut them off from their supply lines!"

Paul laughed. They didn't realize it was just Prellix out there. And there was no supply line. Although—

He forced himself to his feet and hopped on one foot back to the ship. If they were going to try to surround Prellix, he wouldn't let them! He could give them a nasty surprise. There couldn't be more than a few of them, so he could try to pick them off from behind when they didn't expect it and, if he were lucky, not give himself away. And save his sister.

While there wasn't another gun, there was a flare signaler, which Prellix had warned him many times should not be fired near anyone's face. Well, he would decide not to heed that advice. He laughed. He would fire it very close to their enemies' faces indeed. Prellix couldn't be mad at him when it helped her defeat their enemy and take their ship.

He stopped for a second, worried. He shouldn't kill all of them. Prellix had made it clear that the whole point of this was to get one of them to tell the AI to let them have control of the ship. He'd make sure to leave one alive. No more missing dinner for him! Now that he thought about it, the flare signaler probably didn't kill you anyway, just blinded you and maybe knocked you out? He wasn't sure.

He got the flare signaler out of the emergency closet and hopped back out of the ship and toward the noise.

The man was yelling, "We've got her on the run! Loose the barrage."

Paul heard the strange whooshing and thwacking again. Prellix ran into the small clearing and yelled something that Paul couldn't make sense of. He held up the signaler to show Prellix he had a plan, and then something hit him in the chest. He saw a man he didn't recognize run toward him holding an odd bent stick with a wire and another long stick with a knife on the end.

"Paul! Run!" Prellix yelled.

Paul wanted to run, but instead he found himself on his knees without meaning to be. The strange man threw the long stick with the knife at Prellix, hitting her in the back. She yelled and fell down. Damn it. They'd pay for that. He needed her to get back up. Whenever he felt down, Prellix always showed him something or said something to get him excited. If she knew he had figured out a secret attack plan, that would get her excited! Then she would get back up! He tried to show her the signaler gun but immediately realized his plan probably wouldn't work now, because the man, who must be the man the Matriarch had told Prellix about, had seen it too. He wouldn't let Paul get close enough to use it and would probably warn the others. This is why he needed Prellix to make the plans. But wait, his plan had worked! She had seen his flare signaler and was moving again. Maybe he wasn't such a bad planner.

Prellix jumped back up on her feet, but right then the man shot something at her, though it seemed very quiet for a gun. But maybe it was a gun. Paul couldn't hear a thing over the roaring in his ears. Prellix clutched her chest and pitched forward on her knees.

Paul tried to yell a warning that the man was swinging the long stick again, but instead of sound, water came out of his mouth. He looked down and it was red. It wasn't water after all. He must be bleeding, probably from the thing that had hit him in the chest. It was still there after all, and just beginning to ache a little. He had been so distracted by Prellix, he had forgotten about it. He needed to help her! She would be so mad if she saw he let this thing get stuck in his chest. He reached down with his hands to pull it out, but then he heard Prellix yell again even over the roar in his ears.

He looked back over to her and was surprised to find he was lying on his side now. When had that happened? Prellix was yelling because the man had stuck the long stick in her belly. That would be hard to fix. Poor Prellix! She'd be laid up for weeks. He wanted to get up and make that man pay, but he was too tired. And now he'd have to do most of the chores if

Prellix was laid up. Well, he did most of them anyway, but now he'd have to do all the chores.

The man noticed him looking and walked over. Paul tried to scream at him for hurting Prellix, but only more water came out of his mouth. Wait, it wasn't water. What was it? He was so tired. Paul lifted the signaler, hoping to maybe get the man to lean down. But instead the man took the bent stick out again and said, "We declare the war over by right of vanquishment."

Paul didn't understand. What was vanquishment? He never felt the second arrow.

VICTORY

PILOT X STUMBLED back to Verity. His shirt wasn't covered in blood. His clothes weren't torn. He had come through the war in quite good shape, possibly the best shape any soldier had in the history of wars in both universes. He was just sweaty. He'd need a shower. He thought of the singing saltwater shower in the singularity storage chamber. It had felt so good when he had used it for the first time in ages back at the hut.

"A saltwater shower will be just the thing," he said as he climbed into the cockpit.

"What have you done?" Verity asked him.

Pilot X smiled. "You're back! What a pleasant surprise."

"What have you done?" Verity repeated.

"Not to worry. We're safe. The war's over." He rubbed his eyes. "We had to declare war. The stakes were too high. We couldn't find the pieces. And they—" He paused. It had been so clear before. "They attacked us!" That was right. He was provoked. "And killed Lal! And they damaged you. And you weren't here to fix yourself. And I was all alone and—" He broke down crying.

Gentler this time, Verity asked, "What have you done?"

"I killed them," he managed between sobs. "She fought. She was trying to take you—but him. He didn't even know. He was broken already, and I killed him. And her. She was down. No longer a threat and I killed them. I killed them both. I—my god, I—and Rel—I'm a murderer—"

He curled up into a ball. He shuddered, but he could no longer tell if it was crying or something else. He waited for Verity to berate him or explain it to him.

Verity said nothing.

It was dark and cold. He wanted to ask Verity to turn on the heat, but he couldn't manage to speak. He assumed she would have turned it on if that system wasn't damaged, but maybe she was angry with him. He was angry with himself. And he should stop. Because it was anger that had gotten him where he was just now. Anger about the senseless killing of Lal. Anger about losing Verity and possibly being truly alone. Anger about the possibility of another Instant being created and him incapable of stopping it because thieves wanted his ship. Anger at having lived while Alexandra had died.

He gave up and fell asleep and woke to a colder, darker ship.

"Verity?" he managed.

"Yes?" she answered.

"Is there heat?"

"That subsystem is offline. I suggest getting blankets from storage."

She didn't sound mad. But she never sounded like any kind of emotion. "Are you mad?"

"I am unable to be mad."

"If you were able to be mad, would you be mad?"

She paused. She never paused. "You should have waited for me to come back online. A simple diagnostic would have given you an estimate. You requested no diagnostic."

He had given up on her. He started to make excuses about the thieves coming, but they hadn't been. He'd gone to them. He didn't set up defenses; he declared war.

He made himself get up. "What do I need to do to—"

"You don't need to do anything. All repairs can be made by my maintenance systems. Just rest."

She was mad.

Pilot X woke stiff. He had found a warm corner in the singularity storage and covered himself in blankets, the top one showing scenes from an old Alendan children's story. Pilot X had never been a huge fan of it, and he couldn't remember the name. He started to ask Verity and then remembered she wasn't really speaking to him. She had called it variable responsiveness to nonessential communication, but he knew what she meant.

He shook off the children's blanket and the six or seven others piled underneath it and stretched. He was sweating. He'd overdone it, worrying about being cold. He stumbled forward to the food area to look for coffee, but they were out. The pie from Vagson was gone too. Where had that gone? Verity could take items and re-form them for other uses, and she likely needed new materials for her repairs. But why choose to convert the pie? She was mad.

"Verity, do we at least have any juice?" he asked before stopping himself. She didn't respond. Because it was nonessential. He could look in the cooler himself. And he did. And they were out. Well, not technically out. There was a jar from somewhere with a small splash of juice at the bottom and also a pineapple in a stay-fresh vac-pac. He couldn't bring himself to break the seal and eat the pineapple. It was from the Pineapple Planet and while he knew pineapples still existed, he wasn't sure if the planet did.

He sighed and sat down in the middle of the floor. He was a damaged instrument. He was the tool the universe had once needed to fix itself. It made him press the reset button and it didn't need him anymore. If the universe was under threat again, it would need a new tool, not this one. This broken one didn't need to be thrown out, just set down in the back of the shed away from the useful ones.

"Verity, ETA on flight readiness," he said.

"Ready for flight under minimal-needs condition. One-hundred-percent flight readiness shortly."

He smiled. Shortly. She was at least still trying to grow.

"Ready course to Alenda," he said.

"I'm sorry. Return course to the planet at the same coordinates as Alenda?" she asked. It wasn't snotty. If he had to guess, it was shocked.

"Yeah. Take me back to my hut. I'm done."

"Would you like alternate options?" she asked. It was as close as she would get to contradicting him.

"OK," he said, mostly because he missed talking to her.

"We could return to Parthian Prime and pursue the Matriarch. We could return to Parthian Prime and pursue other information sources. We could return to Vagson and retrace steps. We could . . ."

Pilot X waited. "Yes? We could what?"

"Systems fully restored."

"Oh good. And does that mean you'll take me back to my hut now?"

"Alert."

"Oh—come on, Verity."

"Alert."

"Fine. Acknowledged."

"A time tremor has been detected. Its signature matches the first. Shall I attempt to locate it?"

"What? Yeah. Yeah." He stood up.

"Combining data from first tremor and second. The likely origination point is a planet known to Parthian Prime as Koheq."

"You included Parthian Prime's worthless information in your projections?"

"Not in the projections. Only to source the planet name."

"Oh."

"We can find the device without relying on external information sources. With the data we have, proximate scans can detect the device within stellar systems without needing it active."

"In other words, we could fly to Koheq, do another scan, and find it?"

"Yes."

"Verity?"

"Yes?"

"I'm sorry."

"I know. I'm sorry too."

"You can't be sorry. Not really."

"And yet, I really am."

Pilot X smiled. "Let's go find this thing and stop it."

"Preparing for departure, Pilot X."

SECOND ATTEMPT

SHE HAD FIGURED it out. This time it had to work. Just pass this test and she could activate it for real. Then she could properly thank the Order and tell her boss at the Institute. She had overlooked a wiring fault before, which caused a feedback mismatch in the primary conduits. No wonder it failed. Though she still was convinced she had seen a shimmer. Nevertheless, this time it had to work. She could not stomach trying to troubleshoot this mess again.

The lights glowed. The fan hummed. The switch on the Time Rip Regenerator was ready for her test. The main ripeon tuner was still not active. This would just send out test waves.

She flicked it.

A shimmer. She was sure this time. And then?

She glanced down at the screen that showed the test readings.

Greens.

She slumped. This time in relief.

She sighed. Tomorrow she would save her planet. She was no longer at the end of her rope. She couldn't wait to tell her boss. He would be so pleased with her. But not yet. Not until she'd done it. Just in case.

She gathered up her things and made her way down the hall and outside. The air was unusually cool.

Outside was the old man, sat in his usual seat.

"Don't you have a coat?" he said.

"Oh right," she said, and then walked back down the hall. She was so excited about making Trigor work, she was getting absentminded.

She sighed. Again. Tomorrow would be wonderful.

BETRAYED

"YOU CHEATED ON me! Then you gave up on me!" Alexandra screamed.

That wasn't like Alexandra. She was a calm person. A selfless person. Pilot X tried to explain. "No, the Matriarch flirted with me—"

"Not her! That woman! That frozen savage!"

"No, I didn't. I slept on the floor—"

"And then you became a murderer." Alexandra moved closer, her face now grim with the hint of a smile. "I sacrificed myself for the good of Alenda and you saved yourself so you could become a murderer." She was almost smiling now. "And you wanted to give up, you weak fool. You wanted to go back to your miserable hut." This wasn't like Alexandra at all.

"But now we found the signal. Now—"

Alexandra grabbed him by the arms, but she wasn't Alexandra anymore. She was the Secretary.

"Coward. You thought you could defeat my plan, but you can't. You're not even committed enough to stay on the case unless Verity tricks you with an alert."

Now Pilot X was angry. "It wasn't Alexandra. It was never her! It was you!"

"Yes, it was me. You never killed me. Not me. You'll never escape me, either. I'm with you forever. In the place in your heart that should have been kept for Alexandra. I'm there staring at you because you didn't just become a murderer, Pilot X. You've been a murderer since that day on the moon when you first turned on the Instant. Murderer X. That's your profession now. That's why you really don't want to stop the Instant this time. You *want* more people to die!"

"No. That doesn't make sense. No. You're the murderer. And I stopped you. And—"

"Good! Stay confused. Stay weak. Good!" The Secretary pushed Pilot X down on his knees. "Good boy. Stay down. Stay out of it. Stay guilty. Stay sad. It's good. Good!"

"No, it's not—"

"Good morning," said Verity. "We have arrived at Koheq."

"Oh," said Pilot X, now wide-awake. "Good."

KOHEQ

KOHEQ WAS AN advanced technological society at the time in which the tremor originated. The Koheqi were new to Pilot X. They hadn't existed in his universe. He wondered what change had caused that. Plenty of civilizations had survived the restructuring of the universe. The Fringe Cascade, the Pantoonians—well, he hadn't checked on all of them, but Verity said many had.

So, what had the absence of the Alendans, Sensaurians, and Progons done to this planet to take it from uninhabited to evolving an advanced civilization? Was it the absence of the Alendans? Did they leave a niche to be filled?

"Verity, what was this planet—you know—before?"

"This stellar system had no inhabited planets. It was not considered worth colonizing, and no significant life evolved."

"What changed?"

"Speculation?"

"Speculate."

"Random initial event perturbation."

"Well, obviously," Pilot X sneered.

"In simpler terms, the chances for life are random. Resetting the initial conditions and running the experiment again gave a different result."

"Luck of the draw."

"It may have been, as you say, akin to the luck of the draw."

"Well, good for the Koheqi. What do we know about them?"

"They devote most of their resources to researching technological advances. They have become one of the most advanced civilizations. It is unclear what drives them. Most of this information comes from the Parthian Prime public databases, which emphasize trade relations over most other observations."

"Let me guess, humanoid?"

"Yes, humanoid."

"Remind me about that later. I have a project I want to start."

"Ninety-eight percent of people listed in Parthian databases are described as humanoid."

"Great. Remind me of another project I also want to—"

"Exploration of the origins of humanoids logged as pending."

"And as excellent as it is that you knew that's what I wanted, it's impolite to not let me finish."

"Koheq is a cosmopolitan spacefaring race with fewer motivations to examine newcomers than the Parthians," Verity said.

Pilot X opened his mouth to admonish her for changing the subject but decided to drop it. Changing a subject to avoid an argument was in fact a positive development for Verity.

"Can we land?" he said instead.

"We should be able to arrive under an exploratory badge and dock without papers."

"So where are we headed?"

"The Koheqi have outposts on all habitable bodies in the system, but it is likely the development and testing took place on Koheq itself. I can use the signatures of the time tremors to scan for secondary indicators now that we're here. Should we proceed to Koheqi orbit for maximum scan sensitivity?"

"There's only one way to find out."

"Only one way to find out what?"

"If they are the first place to have coffee *and* pie. Head to orbit."

"That doesn't make sense."

"To orbit!"

"Heading to orbit."

Pilot X studied the entries on Koheq from Parthian Prime's database. Koheq had millions of towns, each built up around a central research Institute that focused on a few disciplines. Verity had tracked the Instant's signature to a research town on the planet's largest continent. The town was built around the Gallian Institute, focused on exploration, mining, and planetary motion.

Koheqi research towns all had similar layouts. The Institutes dominated the center of the town. According to the database, this was part of Syndra Herelda's plan to spur the pursuit of knowledge. Only a few dozen had been started by the great leader herself, but many imitators followed.

Businesses and non-research services, including city governments, were located in a ring around the Institute. City governments were subservient to the Institutes and really only supervised portions of the town outside the center. Students and researchers often lived on the Institute grounds, while support staff and local businesspeople generally lived in the outer ring of the towns. Sometimes a fourth ring of related industries might spring up as well.

Syndrania, the Gallian Institute's town, had a few light mining-equipment makers in its fourth ring. There was one rocket-prototype tester and a few labs and development centers for exploration-related equipment.

Verity's scans had only identified the town, not a more precise location within it. They decided to investigate what was going on in the industrial fourth ring, since it would most likely have the infrastructure to support the testing and use of the parts of the Instant. The Institute would too, but if you wanted to stay under the radar with a potentially harmful experiment, the light industrial shops seemed like a better bet. It would be easier for parts of the Instant to blend in there among all the machinery than at the Institute, where open inquiry was encouraged among researchers and students.

Pilot X started by visiting some of the cafés in the second ring, where fourth-ring workers hung out. Verity had pointed out that bars in the second ring would be a more popular choice for the workers than cafés with possible coffee, and Pilot X pointed out that Verity was not going and so could enjoy where he parked her.

He had parked her in Syndrania's only space vessel landing zone, outside the fourth ring on the north side of town. A shuttle train took him through the rings toward the Institute at the center. He could transfer at each ring to move by train around the rings to the other side of the town if he needed, but the landing zone had been near the equipment-makers. So he took the shuttle train straight into the second ring.

Walking out of the station, he felt the old panic. What if this time he found the Instant? Could he really stop it? He actually found himself stopped and beginning to turn, to head back to Verity. He imagined his hut and his plastic container. He wanted to wallow again. He could not disappoint or hurt the universe if he was safely wallowing in his hut. Then the dream came back. And the guilt the Secretary in his dream had tried to use against him. He would have to live with what he'd done. He meant the murders, not the Instant. That thought put things in perspective. His actual murder of Rel and the two thieves was something he should feel deeply wrong about. And it put what he had done with the Instant in perspective. They were not the same. He was not a mass murderer. Just a regular one. And he would have to work forever to expunge that guilt. He, as the parliament and high court of Alenda, would sentence himself to that. He would do his best to make this new universe a better place. He was sentenced to fix it. And it started here on Koheq, by finding the Instant and stopping it.

It was a heavy sentence. He would need sustenance. He found a likely café.

And he found victory. Koheq became his dream planet. Because this café had pie. And coffee.

He hadn't even asked what they called it. He pointed at the thing that was obviously cherry pie and the mugs meant for coffee and gave the biggest smile he had ever given in this universe.

Koheqi business operated on a full credit system. Each person's unique facial ID was scanned, and all income and expenses were credited to that account. Once every five years accountings were made and people were deemed in debt or in surplus. Neither was considered a good situation, and if you were too far out of variance, you had to make arrangements with the Institute of Fairness and Contribution.

People in debt needed to figure out how to contribute more to raise income. People in surplus needed to figure out how to spend more to keep their fellow Koheqi in demand.

This was a little more complicated for foreigners, who might just rack up debt and not stick around for accounting. The Koheqi had a system for that, too. They received goods and services from visitors and generally forgave debts as a consequence. If a foreigner took advantage of the looseness of the system, they would find themselves afoul of the Institutes and be expelled. Any foreigner could be expelled for any reason at any time by the proper official. This didn't happen very often, since the threat kept most visitors behaving within acceptable parameters.

Pilot X knew he wouldn't meet workers in this café, since he was alone. Only one other person came in after him and they ordered tea and left. That person also didn't look like an equipment worker. A bar farther down the street seemed to be where all the workers had gone when they got off the train. But the bar did not look likely to have coffee or pie. At least not of the quality he was currently enjoying. He'd have to get Verity to stock up before they left.

His pie was gone and only a couple more sips of coffee were left in his mug. He thought about getting more, but his wrist kept buzzing with Verity's tips about where to go to look for clues about the devices. He tapped out a couple of acknowledgments to her and got up to leave.

"Oh, can I get you to bring that mug back, please?" the woman behind the counter said. Pilot X apologized and brought her the mug. For the first time, he noticed something in the café besides coffee or pie. The woman was young, probably in school and working here for spending money. She might know a bit about where people went.

"Do you know where the equipment workers go to hang out?" he asked her. "I'm trying to get a deal for some equipment, and I want to do a little, I don't know—"

"Socializing?" she suggested.

"Oh! Well. Not exactly. I mean, I want to make some business connections."

"Ahhh." She looked amused. "Well, that bar down the street? The one that all the workers were going in? Yeah, that's probably where I'd go. Or the factory itself. You know. Make an appointment?" She smirked. Pilot X decided to just let her have the wrong idea.

"But they don't have pie there."

This made her raise her eyebrows.

Pilot X pointed at the pie in the display case.

"Oh! You mean stuffers! Never heard it called—what you said—before."

THE BAR

THE BAR WAS an old, dingy place, the outside of which appeared to have once been made of chrome if you looked closely. At least, Pilot X guessed it was something like chrome. Inside, the bar was so tarnished and dirty, it appeared black. The barstools were metal and a dingy gray. Along one side of the room were booths with hard, silver-looking backs and dull chrome tabletops. The crowd mostly stood around the bar. Most of them wore dingy gray or blue work suits, but otherwise they were average-looking humanoids just like Pilot X.

He slid into an empty booth and immediately understood why everyone was at the bar. The benches in the booths were not comfortable in any way. They were angled wrong and extremely hard.

He didn't think this was the kind of place that had table service anyway, so he got back up and tried to find a spot at the bar to order a drink. This was already one of his least favorite things to do because of the crowd. He never liked to have to fight to pay someone for something. On top of that, he had no idea what to order. He should have asked the woman in the café.

He noticed most of the people at the bar had short, squat glasses filled about two-thirds of the way up with a dark red drink that looked like wine but bubbled like beer. He accidentally got the bartender's attention before he had really decided what to do.

He pointed at the nearest glass of the dark bubbly drink. The bartender nodded and moved away without saying anything. Pilot X still had no idea what the drink was called. He wanted to ask someone, but that was a sure way to call attention to himself. On the other hand, he needed an icebreaker to start finding out information about places that might harbor the kinds of things that would potentially go in a universe-destroying device.

The man sitting next to him had slick, short black hair and big, wide brown eyes. Those eyes were staring decidedly into his drink.

"Settle a bet for me?" Pilot X asked.

The man humphed. "You selling something?"

"Buying. But leave that for later. I'm not from around here."

"No kidding," the man said dismissively, looking away and back into his dark red bubbly drink.

"That drink you have there. My buddy back home says you have some weird name for it. What do you call it?"

"This some kind of joke?" The man squinted one eye at him. "I'm not interested." He looked back down at his drink again and turned slightly away from Pilot X.

"No, I'm serious. What do you call that?" Pilot X said. The bartender came back and set Pilot X's drink down in front of him.

"Breek," the bartender said. "Though people in Atlantl call it keverly."

"See? Thanks." Pilot X raised the glass to the bartender, who moved back down the bar to help someone else.

"And?" The man looked back at Pilot X. "What's the punch line?"

"You call it breek. It's not that weird, if you ask me. Just not what we call it."

This caused the man to swivel abruptly on his stool toward Pilot X. "You going to try to tell me you're Atlantlian?" He laughed.

Pilot X sneaked a look at his wrist. Verity had sent a picture of an Atlantlian. Bright white with ashen hair, and the one in this picture had an extremely long nose. So Pilot X laughed too. "No. Of course not. We don't call it breek or keverly, that's all."

"Everybody calls it breek, buddy. Even most of the Atlantlians. Keverly is like their"—he waved his hand a few rotations trying to think of the word—"concentrated version or something. Native version, maybe." Pilot X skipped point-ing out that those were two different things.

"We call it breeker," Pilot X lied.

The man stared at him. "I forgot about that. So you're Minstran?"

Pilot X looked at his wrist again. A picture labeled *Minstran* showed a rather ordinary-looking humanoid with the same col-oring and hair as Pilot X and most of the people in the room.

"You late for something?" The man indicated the wrist device. "You keep looking at your chrono."

"Sorry, old habit. No, I'm not Minstran, actually. I'm from offworld." He immediately wondered why he had done that when he could have so easily pretended to be Minstran. It was instinct. It was his approach.

"Explains a lot. Well, welcome to Syndrania." The man raised his glass and Pilot X did the same, not sure if there was more to the ritual. The man drank, so Pilot X did too. The breek tasted like old clothes soaked in honey, strained through a moldy peach, and then mixed with vodka. And yet he kind of liked it all the same.

"Thanks," Pilot X managed not to wheeze. "Breeker is what they call it in Bentria, where I'm from. But we heard it was called something like pit juice or something. Do Minstrans really call it breeker too?" he asked.

"Nah. I was trying to trip you up. Sorry." The man looked kind of sulky. "Thought you were a shiller. Horrible thing to think of a person." He raised his glass again and they both drank. "I'm Lamar," he said. "And you?"

"Pilot X," Pilot X said again, deciding not to come up with a cover name. It was easier to lie when most of what you said was the truth. Plus, he was enjoying imagining Verity's frustration as his approach proved to work once again.

"Wow. Bentrian name?"

"Yep."

"Crazy. I like it. Hey, my buddy's sitting there!" Lamar shouted as someone tried to sit to his left on a stool just vacated by someone else. Lamar motioned for Pilot X to have a seat.

"What brings you to Koheq?" Lamar said it with a soft *q*, almost like *kohetch*.

"Looking for parts for a device my boss wants to make. Some kind of physics thing. I'm told this is one of the best places to prototype such things, given the factories and the Institute. Someone tipped us off that similar parts were shipped here." If he thought of Verity as his boss, then it was all sort of true. "So I thought I'd start asking around at some of the factories."

"Nah. We just crank out stuff. And it's higher capacity than what it sounds like you need. I could see where you'd think that though. You'd have better luck at the Institute. They handle all kinds of small prototypes like you're talking about. If you can get anybody's ear there, that is. But you'd be best to find them offworld, especially if you want to keep the cost down. Parthian Prime's where I'd look for that. Not for the manufacturing themselves, but for finding the best deal."

Pilot X tried not to look disappointed. "Yeah, I've been to Parthian Prime, but they sent me this way." *Sort of.* "I mean, I do need models prototyped. You don't do anything like that in the fourth ring?"

Lamar shook his head and looked like he wanted to spit. "I'll be honest"—he lowered his voice and leaned in a bit— "our manufacturing is crap. Pet projects and such. Vanity stuff, really. Professors want to show off to their colleagues or students or maybe sell a few and look like they have a name or something. Real *name* professors get real deals and don't mess with manufacturing here. About—oh, I don't know—thirty percent of our stuff is necessary for the research. The rest is just for ego."

"Well, thanks for the info. I suppose I should try to get an appointment at the Institute then."

"Ha! I like your optimism Pilot Aches." Lamar slapped him on the back. "Finish that and let's get another round." He held up two fingers to the bartender. Pilot X noticed he only had four fingers. Three and a thumb. Then he noticed that everyone in the bar was the same. His middle finger made him feel self-conscious suddenly. He downed his breek and put his hands in his lap.

"That tough, huh?" he asked Lamar.

"What?"

"The Institute."

"If you want to get anything done in a real amount of time, yes. They say they take appointments from all, and they mean it. They'll take them. But they won't keep them. They keep delaying you until you go away or finally make a connection with someone who can get you a real appointment. The real appointments are called audiences. You need an audience with a tenured professor and then you get stuff going."

"And how do you do that?"

"Know somebody." Lamar shrugged.

"Well, the only people I've met on the planet are you and the woman at the café. And I don't even know her name."

"The stuffer place down the street?" Lamar asked. Pilot X nodded. "That's my sister! I mean, my sister's working there right now. She give you a hard time?"

"A little. I was asking about talking to people about parts and I think she thought I wanted to find a date or something."

Lamar shook his head. "No, she didn't. She saw somebody decent and had to mess with him. That's what she does. You know"—he stopped and drank half his fresh glass of breek—"she knows people. Went to school with a bunch of Institute types. Betcha she could hook you up with an audience if she really wanted to."

"Is there any chance she would want to?"

"Nah. Sorry. She's a hard case."

"Oh well."

Lamar chuckled. "Unless you have a pineapple."

Pilot X smiled.

PINEAPPLE

IT TURNED OUT that pineapples were extremely rare. Only a place as rich as Parthian Prime would ever have them in large enough amounts to put them on a menu in a restaurant. The Matriarch had been trying to impress Pilot X with the pineapple shiggen, but he hadn't even blinked. She must have thought him a cad or eccentric. In any case, Lamar knew a lot about pineapples and he knew his sister, whose name was Glonda, loved them. So he took Pilot X back to the café for a proper introduction.

"You cannot be serious," Glonda said.

"I'm entirely serious," Pilot X said.

"He seems serious," added Lamar.

"He can't be."

"I've even been to the Pineapple Planet," he said, probing a little.

She stopped, stared at him, then went back to wiping down the counter. "Now you're just being ridiculous."

"I have and I have a pineapple that I got on the Pineapple Planet in a vac-pac on my ship. It wasn't grown on the Pineapple Planet itself, of course, because—"

And before he could finish the sentence, Glonda said, almost yelled, "They have no pineapples there!" They both began to laugh.

"How the hell do you know about the Pineapple Planet?!" Glonda said, laughing. "I haven't seen that since I was eight."

The Pineapple Planet, it turned out, was the setting of a Koheqi children's show. Pilot X saying he'd been to the Pineapple Planet was like saying he'd been to fairyland. But Glonda had become obsessed with pineapples because of the show and had tracked down a total of eight bites of pineapple in her life. She could remember every one of them and where she was when she ate them. The idea of Pilot X having a whole pineapple was beyond lavish. The idea that he had been to the imaginary Pineapple Planet was a joke. Except for him, it was a sad reality that no longer existed.

"I will give you that pineapple. A whole one. If you get me an audience."

Glonda shook her head. "I need to see the pineapple first. I mean, really. And it better be more than a bit of skin."

"OK. I'll bring it by tomorrow."

"No good. I'm off tomorrow."

"I could bring it by your house," Pilot X said.

"Hey!" Lamar yelled, looking surprised.

"Settle down, Lamar. He doesn't know. He's not from here. Telling a Koheqi girl you'll go by her house is like saying you'll have sex with her, except not phrased as nicely."

"Oh! Oh, I'm so sorry. Lamar, I never meant . . . I just meant I could bring the pineapple somewhere not here. I mean—"

"It's fine," Glonda said.

Lamar looked less sure it was fine but muttered, "Forget about it."

"Look, if you're serious, we can meet at the bar tomorrow. When does it open, Lamar?"

He shrugged. Still seeming a little bugged. "Eleven, I think."

"OK, so eleven at the Starfish," said Glonda.

Pilot X wasn't sure if he was more surprised to realize he had forgotten to find out the bar's name or that the bar was called the Starfish.

"It's not called the Starfish anymore," Lamar said.

"It's always the Starfish to me," Glonda said.

"She's sentimental," Lamar said, finally loosening up. "It was the Starfish for years, and before that—"

Glonda tried to interrupt him, but he shouted over her. "BEFORE THAT, before little miss Starfish here was born, it was called the Racer's Edge and when our pop went there, it was called Mom's."

"What's it called now?" Pilot X asked.

"The Pie Hole."

"Stupid name," Glonda spat.

"Do they serve pie?" Pilot X was confused.

"No!" Glonda said quickly.

"OK. So I will see you at eleven at the Starfish-slash-Pie-Hole, pineapple in hand."

Glonda just nodded. Lamar patted him on the back in an ominous manner and followed him out front.

"Where you staying?" Lamar asked.

"You're not tripping me up with that." Pilot X laughed. "I'm never mentioning a house again."

"Listen. About that. I know you're not from around here, but, uh—and while you seem like a good guy—"

"I will stay away from your sister," Pilot X said.

"No, no, it's not like that. She's a big girl. I just mean. She's my sister and—"

Pilot X's entire body went on alert. He felt his wrist buzz, but he was afraid to look at it and appear rude. But Lamar wasn't meeting his eyes, so he dared. He read from it word for word. "Your sister is a goddess, Lamar, and anyone would be lucky to have her. That's not why I'm here and I promise you: I just didn't know what I was saying. I respect you and I respect her. You can count on that. Understand?"

Lamar laughed and looked up at him. "Fan of the *Koheq Gang* too, I see! HA! Well, all right. I'll let it pass this time. You just better not be full of it about this pineapple. And seriously. You have a place to stay?"

"I'm good," Pilot X said, not sure what had just happened.

"All right. Sleep under stars, my friend. Sleep under stars."

THE COOLER

"WHAT DID YOU make me say?" Pilot X asked Verity once he was back at the landing lot.

"I found a popular video series called the *Koheq Gang*, which featured a story line very similar to your situation, if more dramatic and dire."

"More dramatic and dire?"

"The protagonist, Helvy, had accidentally insulted the leader of a rival faction and risked his relationship with the leader's brother, who was planning to kill him for the offense. I don't believe your insult was as severe or that Lamar planned to kill you."

"Oh."

"The speech got Helvy out of trouble. I assumed it would resonate somewhat whether he recognized it or not, so I adapted part of it to your situation."

"Huh. Play it for me."

"Of course. Helvy's brother is named Loren and the leader of Loren's faction is a woman called Jella."

A video began playing, showing a man in a leather shirt wearing a tight-fitting cloth cap and holding a gun on an older man wearing a white suit with a tall white formal hat.

The man in the white suit began talking. "Loren. I swear. I didn't know. It's me. It's your Helvy."

"You haven't been my Helvy since the day you joined Rorger's gang," said the man with the gun. "And now this? I'm sorry brother-boy. The ship lands here for you and it ain't an island."

"But I didn't mean it, Loren. It's not like she thinks. Like you think."

"Then why'd you say it, Helvy?"

"I was drunk. And I didn't know where I was, and I didn't know it was her, OK?"

"Aww, tell it to the Institute."

"Listen. Jella is a goddess, Loren, and anyone would be lucky to work for her. But that's not why I'm here and I promise you. I just didn't know what I was saying. I respect you and I respect her. You can count on that. Understand me, Loren? Understand?"

Loren lowered the gun, the music swelled, and the two hugged. Verity stopped playback.

"You thought that would work?' Pilot X said.

"It did work."

"Well. This is why you are the computer and I'm the Alendan, I guess. Now. I have rashly been led to exchange rare fruit for a long-shot connection to the people at the Institute. Though it does seem the most likely place to find whoever ordered those parts. So I need to check on the pineapple."

"The pineapple is exactly in the same condition as the last time you saw it."

"Alendan. Computer. Different," Pilot X said, pointing at himself and the ceiling. He climbed through the circular hatch opposite the pilot's chair and into the storage singularity. He felt the shiver he always got when he crossed the line between local space and whatever this was. Verity had not detected that anyone else had developed singularity storage, and Pilot X thought about that every time he went in.

The technology was extremely stable. It didn't require power. It was just an arrangement of atoms that created the stable wormhole into the pocket universe that was permanently attached to his ship. It was as solid as solid-state got. No moving parts, no electronics, no quantum effects, nothing. But over the long course of Alendan history, a handful of accidents had happened. A powerful blow at just the right angle could alter the mechanics and close the wormhole. And since no Alendans existed, should that unlikely event happen to Pilot X's wormhole, there would be no singularity mechanics around to repair it. Everything in the storage area would be cut off from normal space, possibly forever. That included Pilot X if he was in there when it happened. Which made him realize he needed to stock up on food.

He imagined filling the cooler with cherry stuffers as he opened the door to check on the pineapple. Except it wasn't in there. He opened a cabinet. Maybe he'd just remembered it wrong. Nope not there, either. Had he taken it out and put it somewhere? He had been a little disoriented the last time he saw it. He opened several other doors. No pineapple.

"Verity, where's the pineapple?"

"It's where you left it."

"It's not in the cooler?"

"Correct."

"What?"

"You didn't leave it in the cooler."

"Well, where the hell did I leave it then?"

"Under the frog lampstand."

"What? What frog lampstand? Don't play games with me now, Verity, it's not funny."

"Would you like a verbose description?"

"Oh, so now you get all AI on me?"

"As you said. I am a computer. You are an Alendan."

He had hurt her feelings. He was sort of proud of her. "I'm sorry. I didn't mean it like that. I wasn't thinking about what I said."

"That's the second time today that ignorance about your words has gotten you in trouble. I cannot pull you out of this one, since I am not aware of films revolving around similar situations."

"There's never been any similar situations. There's never been a pilot and a ship's AI that spent a whole lifetime together only to destroy the universe and end up with only each other for true company," Pilot X said.

"Yes. If I were to make a Helvy-like speech to me, that would be a good one. The last time you looked at the pineapple, you forgot you had it in your hand and let it roll away. It actually rolled quite far into the next room and under a frog lampstand in the far corner."

Pilot X smiled. He had just been honest, but it was what Verity had needed to hear. He found the pineapple's vac-pac sitting under the ugliest lampstand he had ever seen. It was meant to be a frog, but it was long and thin and sickly green, with the frog-like thing wrapping itself around the lamp's pole in a very off-putting attempt at what Pilot X could only assume was sensuality. Next to the ugly frog lampstand was a chair in a less sickly version of green. Pilot X plopped down in it to open up the pac and look at the pineapple.

He looked at the pineapple in all its spiny, sweet-smelling glory, then had a horrible thought. In this universe, the Pineapple Planet seemed to be a children's tale, not a real place. Who knows what pineapple really meant to Glonda? She might even be disappointed by this. It might be a word that meant some entirely different kind of fruit on Koheq. He should keep it in the vac-pac. Just in case.

Then he was suddenly struck by the reality of giving away the last pineapple. Well, the last pineapple from his universe. He didn't want to give it away. Coffee, pie, and pineapples were all he had left of his identity. Who knew if he'd ever get a pineapple again?

Why was he hesitating? Someone was creating a weapon that should never be used. Even in a good cause it should never be used. The devastation and consequences were too much. He needed to fix this. The way to do that was to find the person who'd been testing the Instant. To find the tester, he needed access to the Institute. And the price of access to the Institute appeared to be one rare pre-reset pineapple.

He tossed the vac-pac a couple times in his hand and began to whistle. He decided he'd make Glonda give him a bite. Or maybe she could make a pineapple stuffer out of it!

THE TRADE

THE NEXT DAY he got up and went to retrieve the pineapple from the cooler where he had mindfully left it the night before. It was still there. He looked around for a bag. The only one he could find was a cloth bag that said *Alenda-Mart. We've got time to save.* He shook his head. Maybe he didn't miss everything about his civilization. He realized at some point he should take some time and throw out a lot of stuff in the singularity compartment. There were probably more useless memories in there he didn't need weighing him down.

He spent the morning wandering around the second ring. He popped into a couple of cafés to test the coffee, but none were as good as Glonda's and too few of them had stuffers. Of course, he tried a slice in every one that did. He tried to get the clerk in one café to call it pie, but the clerk just laughed and said it sounded dirty.

Eventually it got close to eleven, so Pilot X headed toward the Starfish. He liked calling it the Starfish. The Pie Hole seemed wrong. And then it hit him why. "Sounds dirty," he said to himself. "Glonda thought I was looking for a pickup. Oh. Oh dear. Lamar must have thought I . . . I do owe him another apology, I think."

Lamar was the only one in the bar when Pilot X arrived. He was sitting in one of the awful booths. Pilot X steeled himself and slid in across from him. It wasn't quite as bad as he remembered, but it was far from something he would describe as comfortable.

"Hey, so I just put a few things together, particularly the name of this place and—"

Lamar laughed. "I wondered when that coin would drop. It's not a problem. I wasn't hitting on you. A lot of folks come here because it's a nice place, OK? I figured you were one of them. Never thought otherwise."

"But I thought maybe with your sister and—"

"Again. Just me being brotherly. There's a river. There's a raised footpath. Bye-bye water. Don't give it a second thought. Now sit down. Too early for a breek for you?"

Pilot X stopped himself from saying "It's never too early for a breek," which sounded like the right thing to say but was not what he truly felt at the moment. Instead he said, "Do they have coffee?"

"Probably smarter." Lamar stood up without getting out of the booth and yelled, "Hey, Trill. You got a pot on yet? Perfect. Slug a mug for my friend here and get me a breek, will you? Thanks. You're a gem." He sat back down. "So?" He nodded toward the bag. "That it?"

"That's it." Pilot X started to take out the pineapple, but Lamar stopped him.

"Glonda'll gut me if she knows I saw it first. All in good time. I hope it's worth it."

"In what way?" Pilot X asked.

"That bag looks big. That's a pricey thing in there. My sister knows a couple folks at the Institute, sure. Old school friends. I'm not certain they'll be able to help you though. Neither is she. Just saying. Eyes wide open and all that."

"You're not trying to talk me out of it, are you?"

"Don't you even hint at breathing a word of that to Glonda, my dear baby in the basin! No! Just thinking out loud, is all. You do what you need to do, and don't you change your mind on account of anything I say." He was interrupted by a tall, very thin person with silver-white hair showing up with their drinks. "Aw, thanks, Trill. I coulda come and got it."

Trill set a steaming cup of coffee in front of Pilot X. "No trouble. I wanted to say hi to your friend anyway."

"Hi," Pilot X said, waggling his fingers.

"What's in the bag?" Trill asked.

"Pineapple," Pilot X said.

"Aw, sheesh," said Lamar at the same time as Trill said, "Fine, keep it a secret. Let me know if you need anything."

As Trill walked away, Lamar whispered, "Why'd you go and tell her?"

"Because she'll be way less curious now and WAY less likely to think it's a pineapple."

Lamar leaned back. "Clever. She's gonna see it when you give it to Glonda, though, isn't she?"

"I mean, maybe," Pilot X said, but Lamar was no longer listening. He was standing up in the booth again and waving Glonda over.

"Oh, dear basin baby, why are we sitting over here in these torture devices?" she said.

"What's with the baby and a basin?" Pilot X said.

"More private," Lamar said to Glonda.

"Old folktale," Glonda said to Pilot X. "So?" She nodded toward the bag.

Pilot X pulled out the vac-pac. It was vaguely pineapple shaped but was a dull gray and with some small-type wording stamped on it.

"That's not a pineapple." Glonda smirked.

Pilot X took a deep breath. "This is not only a pineapple. It's an irreplaceable pineapple." He tapped a pattern on the side and the vac-pac opened with a shush sound, a little steam rising out.

Inside was the perfect spiny, leafy pineapple, still as fresh as the day it had been picked.

"You are frelling not serious!" Glonda whisper-shouted while shoving Pilot X in the side and simultaneously leaning closer to the pineapple.

Lamar just gaped.

Pilot X lifted the pineapple out and set it on the table.

Lamar snapped out of it and looked around. "You can't just leave it out like this!"

"Honestly," Pilot X said, looking around, smiling, "all you have to do is tell people it's wax. They'll be more inclined to believe something this rare isn't real. They'll be stunned at how good of a replica it is, and it won't likely be stolen, at least not for the money."

"Well, that's just genius," Glonda said.

"I have my moments. I used to have more of them but—something—never mind. Anyway, I assume this will be an acceptable trade?"

"No," said Glonda.

"What do you mean?"

"I mean this is way overpaying. I know a couple people in low-level research jobs at the Institute. It will get you in the walls, sure, and it's possible they could pass you along to somebody who could help you but—this?" She motioned at the pineapple. "It's not worth this."

"Think you could make a pie out of some of it?"

Glonda gave him a look. Pilot X caught himself. "I mean a stuffer!"

She brightened. "Yeah. I bet I could. Seems sacrilegious somehow."

"You take as much of this as you think is fair to eat or sell or whatever you want to do with it. Then you give me the rest back in the form of pie—er—stuffer. Deal?"

Glonda nodded. "Deal."

"What do I get out of it?" Lamar asked. "I hooked you up here."

"Trill!" Pilot X stood up and yelled. "Two breeks on me. Put the whole thing on my tab."

CONNECTIONS

"WELL?"

Glonda hovered nervously over Pilot X, who swallowed the first forkful of pineapple stuffer and said nothing. He took a sip of coffee. He leaned back in the wire chair and closed his eyes.

Glonda wrung her hands, something she was not prone to do. She finally punched Pilot X in the shoulder, almost knocking him over.

"Stop that!" she said.

"It's heaven," he answered.

"Really?"

"Well, it was."

"Was?"

"Until you punched me."

She punched him again. "I'll keep it here for you in the fresher. You have to get going to the Institute if you're going to make the meeting."

"How do I know you won't eat it all while I'm gone?" Pilot X teased.

"I'd never!"

"What about Lamar?"

Lamar, seated on the other side of the table from Pilot X, just shrugged, took a forkful of pie himself, and shoved it in his mouth. "No promises," he said with his mouth full.

Pilot X just laughed. "Fine. Wish me luck?"

"Good luck," Glonda said sincerely.

"Gwood luck," Lamar said around a second bite.

"Keep him away from that," Pilot X said, pointing to Glonda and then the stuffer.

Pilot X took a spine train, the ones that went from ring to ring. It dropped him off at a station outside the Institute's Mechanical Engineering entrance.

Glonda had gone to school with and remained best friends with an engineer named Franciu, who worked as a parts liaison in materials testing. It wasn't far from the kind of person Pilot X needed to talk to, but she wouldn't necessarily know much about secret projects like a device that could replace space-time. Still, he hoped he could convince her to introduce him to the kind of person who did.

Franciu turned out to be twice as tall as Pilot X. She was originally from a moon and had grown up in different gravity conditions. Her people had technically speciated from the Koheqi, though that was an impolite thing to bring up, as there were some historic and not-so-historic fights over what that meant. The moon was called Riheq, and while it was fine to call Franciu a Riheqi, it was not acceptable to use that as a replacement for Koheqi or imply that she wasn't also Koheqi.

Aside from being tall, she had typical brown skin and dark hair and wore something that reminded Pilot X of denim.

"You must be Pilud Aches," she said, trying very hard to say it right.

"That's me," he said politely. "And you must be Franciu."

She nodded in a way that Pilot X felt meant he had done just as well pronouncing her name as she had his.

"We can talk in a corner seat in the test room, though it's not very atmospheric and it can sometimes be loud. Or we can go to the coffee bar."

"Coffee bar, please," Pilot X said.

The coffee bar turned out to be a smallish room with an automatic coffee maker and a bar with stools. Pilot X took it. It was better than no coffee.

"How is Glonda?" Franciu asked.

"Fabulous. She just baked a pineapple stuffer. Delicious."

This impressed Franciu. "Where'd she get the pineapple? Let me guess." She gestured her hand at Pilot X and raised her eyebrows.

Pilot X shrugged and nodded.

"I—I shouldn't ask." She shook her head and then changed the subject. "Glonda said you had some parts you were trying to source?"

"That's what I told her, yes."

Franciu leaned back and stared at Pilot X over the rim of her coffee. "But that's not the whole story?"

He didn't want to divulge everything he knew at once. Franciu was most likely not the person creating the Instant. He should be so lucky. Whoever was creating it probably didn't know the implications of their research or if they did, had not grasped how much damage it could do. But just in case he was wrong, he went slowly.

"Not quite. I work for a very secretive society that keeps an eye out for technology that, possibly without the knowledge of the developer, could be damaging to the universe." It was true, in a way. If he counted himself and Verity as a secretive society.

"The universe?" Franciu said, sounding as if he had off-handedly mentioned that he was hunting killer clowns.

"Yes. We detected the signature of a device originating on Koheq that if used improperly could rip space-time. We want to advise on it."

"You're full of it," Franciu said, and began to get up. "When Glonda hears about this—"

"Wait, look!" Pilot X had hoped he wouldn't have to show the designs to Franciu. He wasn't certain that the Parthians hadn't manipulated them somehow in ways that he or even Verity wouldn't be able to detect. But if showing the parts kept Franciu from kicking him out and getting him banned from the Institute, then he had to. He'd either get no reaction, an attempt to hide recognition, or astonishment, depending.

Franciu threw a skeptical eye at the designs, but as she looked at them, her skepticism faded, and she started paging through them. "These are—"

"Advanced—"

"No—"

"Dangerous—"

"No—well, maybe, but no—"

"What, then?"

"Familiar." *Jackpot.* "Yeah. I sourced components that could have been used for this. But . . ." She shook her head again. "They were all sourced a long time apart and for different projects. Couldn't have been to make this. Too many different people involved, and I would have heard if they were all collaborating."

"Well, maybe someone is trying to cover their tracks."

"Or maybe you got ahold of a bunch of parts orders to make your story look convincing," she said, looking up from the pages.

"No! Listen. I'm from—" His wrist buzzed. Verity had sent him a picture of something. He showed it to Franciu.

"Well, that's just—that's—that's freaking genius. Either your story is right or you're a genius or you know a genius because—can I look at that closer?"

Pilot X held his wrist in a rather uncomfortable position but showed her how to enlarge the picture.

"We need to show this to Barsly. Come on."

Pilot X had no choice. He followed or he didn't find the answer. He was gambling that Glonda the barista was not friends with someone who worked for an evil mastermind. Franciu's enthusiasm seemed to be that of a scientist with a new discovery, so he went with it.

Franciu practically ran through the Institute's hallways, opening secure doors with abandon, forgetting all signing protocols for her guest until they landed in a roomy office of what appeared to Pilot X to be a middle manager.

"This is Sector Overseer Barsly. Barsly, I'd like you to meet Pilud Aches," Franciu said.

"Pile of what?" Barsly said.

"Pilot X," Pilot X corrected. "It's Bentrian. Listen, I'm sorry to disturb."

"Just show him." Franciu waved her hands at Pilot X.

"Show me what, Franciu?"

Pilot X showed Barsly his wrist.

"Can I make that bigger?"

Pilot X once again endured the discomfort.

"Can I put this on a screen somewhere?" Pilot X asked.

Verity replaced the picture with a net code that was used in Koheqi communications. He showed the code to Barsly, who used it to put the picture up on a screen. It was a 3-D rendering of the Instant. Not an actual picture—though Verity had those, too. Verity had made this one from her own knowledge, using the parts notes from the Parthians as a guide to lend their story some credence. It was just a series of blue lines on a white background, showing the outlines of some odd-looking metal machines interconnecting with one another with various tubes and wires.

"Wow." Barsly smiled. "That is beautiful."

"I know, right?" Franciu said.

"The parts are in such a beautiful combination. They almost look like they would work," Barsly said, tracing the connections with his fingers.

"They do work. They're very dangerous," Pilot X said.

"Just the lines and the symmetry," Franciu said, ignoring him.

Pilot X wasn't sure what they saw. It just looked like a clunky bunch of junk that would wipe out your entire history and leave you stranded and alone in an unfamiliar universe to him. But he wasn't a Koheqi engineer.

"Thank you," Barsly said, smiling at Pilot X. "This is gorgeous. Where did this come from?"

They were interrupted by a blonde-haired woman dressed in neutral business attire and carrying a tablet. She was already talking as she came into the room without realizing Barsly had guests.

"—and I keep telling them that you can't ship that far without experiencing some amount of—oh!"

"Oh!" said Pilot X. It was Alexandra.

She was looking at the screen, not him. "What is this?"

"Pilud Aches here was just showing us his invention," Barsly said.

She looked at him for the first time. He couldn't believe he was seeing her. Her eyes were the familiar deep, stormy blue. Had they always been that stormy? Her hair was cut differently than he'd ever seen it, but it had the same luster. Her face was the familiar oval and her lips called to him like they always had. Hadn't they? Still, he knew those lips. They parted and said, "You invented this?" She was staring wide-eyed at him, not with the look of admiration Franciu and Barsly had, but with stunned recognition.

He could barely speak. "Uh, well, no. I didn't. I was trying to find out if I could be parted. I mean, if parts could be made. Uh—"

She seemed to collect herself. "Well, it's very interesting. I'm so sorry to interrupt. I didn't realize you were occupied."

"It's quite all right, Kayla," said Barsly.

"Kayla?" asked Pilot X.

"I'm so sorry. Yes, I'm Kayla," she said. "I'm a research assistant for Barsly. I'm afraid I didn't catch your name?"

"Pilot X," he said, finally standing. "Nice to meet you— Kayla."

"Pilot X." She said it perfectly. "Pleasure to meet you, too." Then she turned to Barsly. "I'll catch up with you later about the shipping issues?"

"No problem, Kayla."

Pilot X watched her go. Again. But not. No, this was Kayla. Not Alexandra. He shook himself. How could anyone even look like Alexandra? She didn't exist. His wrist buzzed. Verity had noted abnormal bio indicators in Pilot X. He'd explain later. He looked up and realized he was still standing, facing the door and tapping his wrist device.

"Everything OK?" Barsly asked.

"Yes, sorry." He turned back around. "Work stuff." He pointed to his wrist. Franciu and Barsly nodded.

"Well, listen," Franciu said. "Those parts are familiar, but that's as much as I can say, really. Barsly could tell you more."

"I could, yes. But not much more than tell you which divisions could have designed which bits. Honestly, that won't be much help to you. Whoever ordered the parts would have needed to talk to a coordinator. They could tell you what I could tell you, plus help you get quotes and timelines."

"Excellent. How do I go about seeing a coordinator?"

Barsly and Franciu looked at each other. "Well. The old joke is that if you have to ask, you probably can't. But I imagine your boss would know. You see, the Institute is not a commercial enterprise, so there always needs to be a research gain for any project. I could go on, but, suffice to say—it's complicated."

"I'll be honest with you," Pilot X said. "I had to make a connection with Franciu's school friend to get to you, sir. I'm not confident of my ability to get an appointment with a—coordinator—without some help."

Barsly just sighed. Franciu looked at Barsly. "He gave Glonda a pineapple."

"He what? Are you serious? A real pineapple?" He looked at Pilot X. "One would think a person capable of slinging around pineapples would be able to get a coordinator. In fact, if you can get it back, you might be able to use the pineapple to get an audience." He chuckled.

"I'm afraid it's mostly being made into a stuffer right now."

"I would like a bite of that," Barsly said, mostly to himself.

"I could arrange that," said Franciu.

"If," added Pilot X.

"If I help you get an audience," said Barsly. "Although Franciu here is an older friend of Glonda's than you are and Glonda controls the stuffer, I bet."

Pilot X laughed. "Yes, OK. That's true. What are my options?"

"I honestly don't know," said Barsly. "Even if I wanted to, it's not something that's easy for me to make happen."

"Even less so for me," said Franciu.

"Don't give up," Barsly said. "Let me mull on it and Franciu will too, right, Franciu? We'll come up with something. Give us a day."

Barsly's inability to make eye contact as he said this told Pilot X what the answer would be.

"Well, thank you. And I'll see what I can do about making a more direct connection."

Barsly stood and smiled at this, as if Pilot X had said the correct answer. "Good luck," he said.

Franciu walked him out and back through the corridors.

"He's not going to be able to help me, is he?" Pilot X asked.

"No, probably not," Franciu said. "I wish I had a better answer for you."

"I just have to keep plugging away."

Franciu stopped and looked at Pilot X. "If you don't mind my saying so, I get the impression that this is personally important to you. I still don't know whether to believe your crazy secret society story, which is why I didn't bring it up to Barsly, and I noticed you forgot to bring it up too. And whatever it is you're really doing, you're desperate enough to throw a pineapple at a café clerk in order to get a meeting about parts. And where does anyone get a pineapple? Barsly's right. People who can toss rare produce around like that would usually be able to get an audience with a coordinator. They'd just know how. Why don't you?"

"I—" Pilot X wasn't sure how he was going to answer, but they were interrupted by Alexandra. No. Kayla.

"Pilot X," she said. "I was hoping I would catch you. I wanted to ask you a couple more questions about your invention."

"Well, it's not my invention—"

"Franciu, do you mind? I can show him out when we're done."

Franciu shrugged. "Sure. It was nice to meet you, Pilud Aches. Let me know if there's anything else I can do for you. Maybe I'll see you over a stuffer soon." She laughed ruefully and walked away.

"Let's get a meeting room," said Kayla, leading him back through the corridors in a different direction. The Institute's corridor walls were padded, and the floor had thick gray carpeting that kept everything soft and muted. Their footsteps didn't make a sound. There was no one else in the corridor with them. The silence was killing him.

"Kayla? Can I ask you something?" he said.

"Let's just wait to talk until we're in the meeting room," she said, clipped and businesslike.

Could this possibly be Alexandra? Had she escaped? Was she hiding her recognition of him? Was she mad? Was she happy? Was she madly happy? They finally got to a door marked *Secure Room*, and Kayla tapped some controls and the door opened with a *shwoosh*.

With a tight smile, she motioned for him to enter first. It was a padded room with padded chairs and a padded table and several screens. The door closed behind them. Kayla tapped some more controls and a machine voice said, "SECURED."

Pilot X turned.

Kayla slapped him. "Who the hell are you and how did you steal my work?"

"Your—what? YOUR work? You're making the Instant?"

"What's the Instant? Why do you have pictures of the Trigor? Who are you?"

"I'm Pilot X. I'm—well, of course. You don't recognize me."
He said it as a flat statement. This was, despite the uncanny
coincidence, definitely not Alexandra.

"No. I don't recognize you, Pilot X, which is not your real
name. I checked. There is no Pilot X on record. The Institute
has very thorough records on all traders, manufacturers, and
anybody who might likely have an honest reason to come here,
and you're not in their records. Who are you and where are you
from?"

Pilot X sat down in a chair and sighed.

"Answer me! How do you know about the Trigor?!" she
yelled.

"Because I used it before!" he yelled back.

"That's a stupid thing to say. It's not even done. Who are
you and where are you from?"

He was too upset to think now. "I'm Pilot X. I'm from
Alenda. I'm here because I detected the signature of a horrible
weapon called the Instant, which I once used—was forced to
use—convinced to use by—a woman I loved—to prevent the
destruction of the universe."

"You're nuts," said Kayla.

She looked so much like her. He let it all out. "It's why you
can't find records of me. You won't find records of a place called
Alenda, either. It still exists. Just doesn't have any people on it.
Except me. I wiped them out. I wiped all of us out, including
you." He held her gaze, but he was crying.

"What?" She turned as if to go or call someone, then
stopped.

"You know I'm telling the truth, and you want to think I'm
crazy, but you know I'm not," Pilot X said through tears. "And
the fact that you know those things frightens you more than
the fact that I have the specs of your secret project."

"It's not a secret project," she said.

"Barsly didn't know about it. Franciu recognized the parts but not the whole. It was secret from them."

"It's not secret. Just—compartmentalized," she said.

He laughed, wiping his eyes. "Ah. So the weapon that can wipe whole civilizations out of existence is just a compartmentalized project. For security reasons, I suppose," Pilot X said.

"Yes. Well, no. Stop. You're confusing things. It's not a weapon."

"Oh. What is it then?" His grief was changing to anger. A familiar feeling. "A preventative measure? A contingency? A deterrent? I once knew somebody who used it as a myth."

"No! It's our last hope."

"It was mine once too. Let me tell you, it doesn't work out well for the user. Bad design, that."

"I can't tell you any more and anyway, I'm asking the questions here. Why do you know that?"

Pilot X had recovered himself somewhat. "Come with me to my ship and I'll show you."

"Ha! No, thank you. You're not leaving here."

"It's perfectly safe. Check for a ship called *Verity* parked in the landing zone. It's registered. And I can introduce you to a couple of local friends I've made if you want more assurances. You might even get to have a pineapple stuffer."

"Nobody makes pineapples into stuffers," she snapped, confused by the statement.

"I do."

"I do not trust you and you haven't answered my questions."

"I have. You just didn't believe the answers." He couldn't take back what he already had said, so he decided to double down but this time with a calmer explanation. "I once used a device very much like the one you're making. It changed the universe and I was the only survivor—I think—from that version. Myself and my ship, *Verity*. Verity detected the test of your—what did you call it? Trigger? We tracked it here to find out who was using it and why. If you want more, it's at my ship." His wrist buzzed.

He looked down. Verity had sent him a message. He almost lost control again when he saw it. He showed it to her. It was a picture of Pilot X with the Instant as he had been setting it up before activation.

"That's you. But that's—" was all she said.

"Yes. I can show you more. I can maybe help you."

"Help me what?"

"Avoid making a horrible mistake."

"I shouldn't trust you," she said. "I don't trust you. But. . . if I'm honest—"

"Yes?"

"Nobody knows I've been working on the Trigor. It's not just compartmentalized. It's a rogue project. So I guess I have to trust you. Because if Barsly starts telling people what he saw, I'm going to have to have some good answers for what I've been doing."

"You can say that again." Pilot X stood. "Well, coffee, stuffers, and then my ship?"

She threw up her hands. "Fine."

DIPLOMACY

KAYLA SAT QUIETLY, staring at a small slice of pineapple stuffer.

"You're sure you want to give her a share of it?" Glonda said skeptically. "She doesn't seem to want it."

"I'm sure," was all Pilot X said.

Finally Kayla took a bite. "Wow."

"Wow?" Glonda said sarcastically.

"It's really pineapple. You didn't lie about that."

"He hasn't lied to me about anything," said Glonda. "To be honest, we just met him, so what do we know? But he's meant everything he said to me, and he hasn't lied."

"Well, yeah, I did," Pilot X said.

"Not helping," said Glonda.

"I told Lamar I worked for a secret society. The society is just me and my ship. But other than that, everything I told them and everything I told you, Kayla, is true."

"And you've told me everything?" Kayla said.

"No," said Pilot X. "For that, we'll need Verity."

"Then we should get going," Kayla said, standing up.

"Oh, don't. You only just got here," Glonda said flatly while whisking away the dishes and coffee cups. "You'll be all right?" she said to Pilot X with more seriousness.

"I'll be fine."

They rode the shuttle to the landing lot in silence. He just looked at Kayla. He tried not to stare. She occasionally caught him looking and he looked away every time. He couldn't fathom it. The Koheqi weren't Alendans. They were close. Both were the typical bipedal mammals that were common in his universe and seemed to dominate this one. The Koheqi shared the Alendan-like characteristic of pursuing knowledge, but that was about it. Koheq did not develop time travel, nor did the Koheqi think they were in charge of space-time.

And yet here was Alexandra. By every outward appearance it was her. Same eyes, same hair, same face. Same voice. Same everything, except name, occupation, and memory. What would Verity say? Verity must know already. She would have recognized the voice, if nothing else.

They arrived at the landing lot.

"That's your big ship?" Kayla asked.

"It's bigger than it looks," he said.

"Is it?" She very much did not sound convinced.

"One way to find out," he said, and climbed in, motioning for her to follow. There was room for about four to five adults in the main compartment in addition to the pilot.

"I see what you mean." She shrugged.

"He means my singularity storage chamber, available from a hatch at the aft," said Verity.

"Oh!" Kayla said, surprised.

"Verity, meet Kayla, Kayla, Verity."

"Hi," said Kayla.

Verity did not respond.

"Be nice, Verity. Let's go through here," Pilot X said, opening the hatch to the singularity chamber.

"Leaving already?" Kayla said, presuming it was an exit.

"Not exactly!" Pilot X yelled from the other side, his voice echoing.

Kayla poked her head through. All Pilot X heard was a quick inhale.

"Is this—does this go on—what is this?"

"It's a singularity. It exists in its own pocket universe. It's Alendan tech. Nobody in existence that we know of can do it. We're pretty wrecked if it ever gets broken. But it's also pretty stable. Doesn't need to be maintained to exist. Just keep proper alignment—"

He stopped because he could tell she wasn't listening anymore.

"How big is it?" she asked.

"It is very large," Verity said, practicing her new talent of not giving precise measurements.

"Funny, Verity," Pilot X said.

"It's stable?" Kayla asked.

"Yeah. Once it's pried open, it stays unless you do something to collapse it. Pretty stable."

"How do you open it? This is fascinating. I've spent a lot of time studying singularities, but I never thought I could be near one, much less walk through one."

"Not all singularities are black holes."

Kayla looked annoyed. "Yes, I know. But I still never thought I'd be near one, even a Bridge-Tunnel Invariate."

"A what?"

"Oh look. Poor alien is confused," she mocked.

"A Bridge-Tunnel Invariate is the Koheqi label for the type of singularity we use on the ship," Verity interrupted.

"Thanks. I'd sort of gathered that." Pilot X scowled.

"Slow and steady wins the race," Kayla said.

"All right. I'd love to explain more about how this works, and I will. But first things first. Verity, we need to show Kayla more pictures—from that day."

"You mean the day you used the Instant to—"

"Yes, Verity, that day."

He guided a distracted Kayla to a screen and pulled over a couple of chairs.

Verity began playing a video. Pilot X turned away. He couldn't watch. He could tell when it was done because Kayla turned around to look at him.

"You had to do it," she said, sounding just like Alexandra.

"That's what you said."

"I—but. I can see. You had to. And that's my machine." She shrugged. "There're no two ways about it. You invented it first. Then I did."

"I didn't invent it," Pilot X said. "It was made by my people, though. It was ancient when I used it, or at the time I used it and in relation to me."

"Time travelers," she said, for the first time sounding like she admired something he'd been part of. He drank the admiration in like juice on a hot day. "It must be incredibly complex to live outside of time. It's one of the things I've had to consider with Trigor, but not on the level you're talking about."

"Now that you've seen what I've been talking about, do you believe me? Do you trust me?"

"I think I believe you," Kayla said. "I'm not sure I trust you."

"I'll take it. What I need to know from you is why you are building this. What good could it possibly do?"

"I'm going to tell you something most people on Koheq don't know. The people who do know don't believe anyone else should know. I don't trust you, but you've taken me into your confidence, so I'm willing to take you partway into mine, especially because you're not Koheqi. Can I trust you not to tell anyone? Not Glonda. Not Lamar. Not anyone."

"You can trust me," Pilot X said.

"Specifically, not to tell anyone?" she pressed.

"Specifically, not to tell anyone."

"An anomaly has opened near our solar system. We often call it a gravity well, but that's just an effect. It's some kind of rip in space-time. It's small now, but eventually it will destroy Koheq."

"We didn't detect any anomaly when we arrived. But we weren't looking for one either," Pilot X said.

Verity interrupted. "I detected it but did not mention it because it was inconsequential to our arrival."

"Fine. So, it's there," Pilot X said, trying to suppress his annoyance at Verity not telling him. "Why destroy the universe over it?"

"The Trigor does not destroy the universe. It fixes rips in space-time."

"I don't know. Trigger sounds like a weapon to me."

"Not Trigerrr. Tri-GOR. It stands for 'Time Rip Regenerator.'"

"Oh. You're trying to harness it to fix the anomaly!"

"Yes! Congratulations! You win the prize for understanding what I've been trying to tell you since I slapped you," Kayla said.

"Oh. That was on purpose?"

"That was very on purpose!" They were shouting now for some reason, and in each other's face.

"Why are you yelling?!"

"I don't know!"

"I do," Verity interrupted

"SHUT UP!" they both yelled in unison.

After a few moments to catch their breath, Pilot X continued. "You can't fix the anomaly with the Instant. Or Trigor or whatever you call it."

"How do you know?" she asked.

"That's not how it works. It rewrites time. All time. You can tell it to do really broad things and those things will have some pretty crazy repercussions, as I'm finding out. But you can't use it to fix a rip in one place. I mean, I suppose you could try, but you might wipe out the entire Koheqi civilization in doing so, or more likely alter it in a way that makes it unrecognizable. It's like blowing up a building to kill an ant."

"But if we don't try, we'll all die anyway."

Pilot X was about to tell her how that did not justify replacing the rest of the universe but was hit in the gut by a softball of guilt. It was what he'd done. Maybe for a much more urgent reason, but it was what he'd done. Then he had another thought.

"Maybe your people figure out another way. Let's find out," he said.

"Find out what?" She frowned.

"What happens to Koheq."

"What do you mean 'let's find out what happens to Koheq'? You mean just wait around for centuries to watch it fall into the rip? Besides the fact that I'll be dead—"

"Timeship!" Pilot X pointed up. He wasn't sure exactly why he pointed up instead of any other direction, but she seemed to get the point. "We go look. Verity!" he said, leaping back through the hatch into the pilot's seat. "Take us up, out of orbit, and ten thousand years into the future. That ought to be enough, yeah?" He turned to see Kayla standing with her arms crossed just inside the cockpit. "You'll want to strap in. It's usually smooth but just in case. Don't want you bouncing off the ceiling."

Pilot X didn't bother to check if she followed his advice. He was too excited. If you'd been sitting there and asked him why he seemed so excited, he would have been hard-pressed to say. It might have been the pleasant fiction that he was flying in Verity with Alexandra. It might have been the simple thrill of a timeship mission to fix something. Going to a point in space-time to confirm an anomaly had once been his main occupation. It was probably both of those plus the distraction of not doing something directly related to the Instant. Whatever it was, he didn't give it a passing thought but just enjoyed the feeling.

The ship shuddered and left Koheq, shooting out of its gravity well and into free space, away from planetary bodies and slightly above the ecliptic. Deciding to add a flair of drama for Kayla's sake, Pilot X said unnecessarily, "Engage quantum-splitter drive for time shift!"

"Drive was already—oh." Verity caught up with the irrelevance of the statement and said nothing more.

There was the slightest shudder. Kayla might have described it as almost a shimmer. Nothing inside the ship changed, but the view outside changed dramatically. Koheq's star was gone and everything was dark. The stellar system had disappeared.

"Engaging external lights," Verity said. She never said the word *engaging* like that. Pilot X was almost sure she was making fun of him.

A flood of light poured out of the ship and reflected off a thin scattering of debris. Not much was left. What was still there trailed out in spiral arms from a central point that was the rip.

"How's our position?" Pilot X asked.

"Advise moving soon. The shift positioned us on the edge of the rip's event horizon."

"Take us up and out, then get ready for calculation." Pilot X was all business now. Caught in the procedures of arriving somewhere dangerous and then adapting.

He heard Kayla say, "I had no idea. I mean. It makes sense. But it's . . . it's gone." He found a natural place in his work to pause, knowing Verity would keep them safe, and turned to look at her. She was broken. Tears streamed down her face. Her mouth hung slack like a child who had broken a favorite toy and had no hope of ever seeing another again. It was that expression times one million.

He had simultaneous urges to hug her and to laugh. He wanted to hug and comfort the person who looked like Alexandra, because her face showed so much pain. He wanted to laugh and tell Kayla that if she was upset about this, to wait until she saw what her Trigor did to all of existence. Instead he said, "Verity, plot the point when the rip would envelop Koheq and take us to say fifty years before that."

"Why?!" Kayla yelled.

"To show you what's there. To show you what your people do with the knowledge you have once they all know. Just—just watch."

It was a gamble. But before he could change his mind, he felt the shudder that meant the jump was done. The stellar system was back. It didn't immediately look odd to Pilot X, but Kayla was moving toward the viewports. "It's dark. They're all gone." He saw what she meant. There were no lights of cities on Koheq's surface.

"There is a system-wide broadcast being repeated. Would you like to hear it?" Verity said.

"Yes, please," Kayla said, almost as a whisper.

A strong baritone voice began speaking: "*Warning. This stellar system is unstable and collapsing into the Koheqi Rift. All agencies advise no entry. There is no remaining salvage on Koheqi settlements. Koheq has relocated to star system 127665D6544RJ in the standard system, which also goes by the local names Gravell or Bentria. You can contact Koheqi emigration authorities there for further information. Warning. This stellar system—*" Verity stopped playback.

"Should we go to Gravell?" Pilot X ignored the use of the made-up name of his made-up planet for the time being. "So you can see how the future Koheqi have survived without having to blow up the universe?"

"This means you stop me."

Pilot X raised a finger, opened his mouth, and closed it again. Then said, "Yes and no. That's kind of the trick of something like the Instant. Or the Trigor. It works by replacing the timeline so the original no longer exists. That means we would no longer exist, and this never happened. We're overwritten, you might say. We're never going to see evidence of that happening because once it happens, we will no longer be around to ask the question."

"But we're here now. Wouldn't we feel ourselves disappearing or something? What happens to this time we're in now? These events?"

"They literally never happened," Pilot X explained. "I know it's odd to think about when they're happening right now and you're in them, but you're privileging your perspective from inside. From outside of time and space it's like you poured some water on a paper with watercolor. It just disappears, and you can't get it back. You especially can't get it back because time—is affected. Oh, it's really hard to explain, I know. But think of a big cube full of pieces of paper with numbers on them. If you're looking at a number, you know you can go down in the cube and get another number. And even if you destroy the paper, you know you can get to the point in the cube where the paper was. But if you destroy the cube? It's all gone."

"That didn't make any sense at all."

"OK, think of a flower—"

"Forget it. I can't realize it, but I understand. Despite my being in it, it can be destroyed and then my being in it is gone too."

Pilot X snapped his fingers. "You've got it."

"So it won't matter if I try."

"Wait. What? No!"

"I can try to use the Trigor to repair the rip. If I fail and it does not act like you say, Koheq will survive in some way. If I fail and existence is replaced, none of what we're doing matters because it was never the real timeline anyway." She almost smiled as she worked this out aloud.

"No! No, no, no. It's not fate. You can choose to keep existence or not."

"You chose." She turned on him, smiling. "That's what you said. You chose to wipe out your existence. You made that choice for others. And now I see why. Nothing lasts afterward. There are no consequences, because even consequences are eliminated because the things that caused consequences never existed."

"Except me. I exist. I am the consequences. I carry the consequences with me every single moment!"

"Well, I can solve that for me. I just have to be outside the protective field when it goes off. Then nobody will be left to carry the consequences if it fails."

"This is not where I expected you to go with this at all."

"Take me back. I have to get to work."

"No. Just wait—" But Pilot X felt the shudder and then the motion as Verity returned them to their original time point and began the descent to Syndrania. "Verity, where are you going?"

"She requested to be returned to her work. I am returning her. It would be a violation to involuntarily restrain her."

"It's not restraint—Kayla—wait."

But by the time he could collect himself, Verity had landed, and Kayla had already opened the cockpit door and was walking away. She turned and said, "Thank you, Pilot X. Thank you for showing me time and freeing me to do my work. I'm sorry I was angry with you. Good-bye."

And then she was gone.

CONSEQUENCES

"WHY DID YOU do that?" Pilot X said, slumped in his pilot's chair.

"She was distraught. You should not have showed her the destruction of her world. She was not prepared. It was best to honor her wishes and try again to reason with her once she's calmed down. If she calms down."

"What do you mean 'if'?"

"She seemed to be an excitable young woman."

"Well, we better hope you're wrong."

"Yes, our alternative action would be most unpleasant."

"Alternative action?

"Elimination."

"What? Kill her?"

"If necessary," Verity said.

Pilot X's blood ran cold. He would not do that again to anyone. Certainly not to Alexandra. He stopped himself. Or Kayla. "When have you ever recommended killing?"

"There been several battles where I have recommended strategies that could lead to death or damage—"

"When have you ever recommended killing a civilian?"

"She is not Alendan. Her pursuit of the Trigor, despite our advice, is an act of aggression against all of existence."

"You *really* don't like her."

"You think she's Alexandra."

"Oof. Wow. I—"

"She is not Alexandra. Alexandra is no more. She exists only in your memories. This physical copy is not her."

"Who turned on your mean program?"

"Practical truths can sometimes appear harsh."

"Harsh? You recommended killing her."

"I recommended persuading her to stop. I admitted alternative plans could require elimination. Not all forms of elimination would result in death."

"What forms of elimination do not result in death?"

"Removal with a possibility of return indistinguishable from zero."

"Kidnapping."

"As an example."

"We're not kidnapping her. And we're not killing her."

"She is a threat and the Trigor must be destroyed, along with the knowledge for building it."

"I have that knowledge," he said. "I built the Instant from plans Alexandra helped me get. I'm just as much of a danger."

"You are an exception. The likelihood of you rebuilding the Instant and using it is near zero."

"Ah, but not indistinguishable from it?"

Verity paused before answering. "No."

"What would you do if I tried to rebuild the Instant?"

"I would follow the same path of actions we are following now regarding the Trigor."

"And you'd consider killing me?"

"I would avoid that option if at all possible."

"But not for her."

Verity paused again. When Verity paused, she wasn't thinking. She wasn't at a loss for words. Pilot X knew this. She was recalculating. Checking her work millions of times on the off chance there was an error. It was the machine intelligence equivalent of doubt. Eventually she said, "I would avoid that option if at all possible."

"For me," he said.

"She is not Alexandra."

Pilot X noticed Verity's deft use of a change of subject. So he called her on it. "Don't change the subject on me."

"Apologies. It was not meant as a change of subject. I merely forwarded through the logical steps that you would have taken to get to a defense of Kayla, despite the fact that she is a direct threat working actively on a device that could destroy us all. I believe one factor causing you to defend her is her resemblance to Alexandra. So I jumped to pointing out the very obvious but important fact that, despite her appearance, she is not Alexandra."

"She's also not the Secretary. Remember him? The one whose plan caused me to rewrite the universe? Ring a bell? She's not him. She's not hell-bent on destroying the universe."

"She will not consider the consequences of her actions," Verity said. "You have tried reason. It did not work."

"Only because she saw her home destroyed. That was my mistake. I was trying to show her how they survived. I—never mind that. I don't blame her. What if we can save Koheq in another way?"

"The only way to save Koheq would be to remove the rip."

"Can it be destroyed?"

"Unlikely. The power needed to do so would be difficult to come by and would likely also destroy the rest of the stellar system."

"Can it be closed?"

"It could be collapsed given the proper stimulus."

"What stimulus would it need?"

"It is a space-time anomaly. A properly calibrated pulse could collapse it at its origin point, without needing much energy."

"You mean go back in time?"

"I mean go forward in time."

"Wait, why forward?" Pilot X was confused, a state he found himself in more often these days. Side effects.

"The pulse would need to run backward through the majority of the rip's history to be effective."

"Why couldn't we pop back in time to the moment it first appeared and just pinch it closed somehow?"

"It does not exist in normal space-time. When it is smallest is not its beginning. To pinch the rip closed, you would have to hold it closed throughout time. A pulse directed backward in time would be simpler and require less energy."

"What kind of pulse?"

"A charged chroneon pulse would work."

"The only thing that can create a chroneon pulse is the Instant."

"The Instant would provide too great a pulse for that narrow of a purpose. Hence the problems with Kayla's Trigor."

"Is there a way to modify the pulse?"

Verity paused. "There is no way to modify the pulse with the Instant."

"What about the Trigor?"

No pause this time. "The designs are the same. There is no way to modify a pulse with the Trigor."

"Wait, but I asked if there was a way to modify the pulse at all, not a way to modify the pulse with the Instant or the Trigor. Is there?"

"A chroneon pulse could conceivably be modified."

"How?"

"By creating a field modulator as a pass-through to the main pulse between generation and dispersal."

"Hold on. Could we create an addition to the Instant—or the Trigor—to do that?"

Verity paused. It was a long pause. Pilot X was worried she was broken. He was about to repeat the question when she said, "Yes."

"WHAT?! You knew this?!"

Less of a pause this time. "Yes."

"When did you know this?'

"I surmised it as part of a thorough analysis of the Instant the first time you showed it to me. It was unnecessary for the purpose of ending the Secretary's plans, which involved a much wider purpose of—"

"I know what the purpose was. So we could modify the Trigor?"

"No."

"No, not modify. We could create something—an add-on—that would modify its output?"

"Yes."

"So it's not a threat to the universe."

"As currently constructed, it is."

"But it could be made safe!"

"Even with an add-on, it could pose a danger if improperly used."

"So could your quantum-splitter drive. But we have safeties. Let me get this straight. You've always known the Instant could be modified to be less dangerous. So when you detected the—the Trigor—you knew the limits of it as a threat. You could have told me that then."

"You were wallowing. You needed to get out more."

"And . . . And . . . if we had developed this add-on before—when you first knew about it"—Pilot X was hyperventilating—"we could have saved my people *and* the universe. We could have eliminated the war without everything else being affected!"

"Unlikely. The target was too wide and intertwined."

"But it's possible!" he shouted.

"Incalculable. Stop looking like that. I'm not letting you park me forever on that planet again."

Pilot X stormed out.

LOST

HE HAD NO idea where he was going. It was raining lightly outside. He found himself wandering through the residential ring and got lost. He could occasionally see the Institute's buildings through the trees, and he knew if he kept wandering toward them, he'd eventually hit the ring transport network. But where would he go? Glonda and Lamar wouldn't understand all this. He couldn't fly anywhere without talking to Verity, and he didn't want to talk to her again anytime soon. He could try to see Kayla, but that was hopeless. Even if he could penetrate the Institute's security, she probably wouldn't agree to see him.

So he walked in the rain. Eventually he got to a transport stop. Across the way was a row of shops and restaurants. Instead of hopping on a shuttle, he just kept walking, and wandered into a toy store. There were no kids in it at the moment, but the objects were colorful small models of Koheqi things. There were a few versions of the Institute in miniature. There were several dolls of prominent researchers. Was it a toy store or a collector's shop? Either way, the shopkeeper very obviously did not like the wet, bedraggled man who was stalking his aisles, so Pilot X left.

He went a few doors down to a clothing store, but he felt no more welcome there. Though they did have raincoats. He was about to ask about them when realized he didn't want to speak. Not to Verity. Not to the shopkeeper. Not to anyone. He left the shop without saying a word, and walked some more.

He thought about the war. He thought about the Ambassador who'd given him his first job. He thought about building a hut on ancient Alenda. He thought about Guardian Lau's party. He thought about the Instant. Mostly he thought about his last conversation with Alexandra. How it was she, the one person he might have actually cared about, who convinced him to destroy her and everyone else. He thought about that moment. The flick of the switch. How he had thought at first it hadn't worked. How it had worked horribly. How he fled to the Fringe Cascade. His trial. How he had fled from the Fringe Cascade. How Verity had finally awoken him from his stupor with a threat. How Verity cared that much about him even if she was an AI. How Kayla cared that much about her people.

He found himself at the Institute. He knew he had meant to come here all along. The wandering was just a subconscious way to stop himself from worrying about what he would do when he got here. And now he was here.

He was standing, just staring at the entrance, when Franciu happened to come out.

"Pilud Aches? I didn't realize you'd made another appointment?"

"I haven't, Franciu. Can you help me?"

She wrinkled her brow and pursed her lips but did not say no.

"I need to see Kayla."

"Does Kayla want to see you?"

"I have something important she needs to know."

"Okay," Franciu said slowly. "And you can't come back later?"

"I'd rather not."

"Fine." She scowled and seemed to come to a decision. He hoped it was the right one. "I've been thinking about those diagrams and . . . she needs to deal with this. Come with me."

She took him back through the door, gripping his arm a little painfully, and dragged him to the coffee room. He had a hard time not asking her if he could have some coffee. She noticed.

"Oh, sparkling stars, get yourself some coffee. And wait here. I'll be right back."

The coffee was a welcome escape. He hardly noticed time had passed when Kayla came into the room. She was so much like Alexandra. Every time he thought he had gotten used to it, she looked at him and he crumbled inside.

"Franciu said I should listen to you," she said. "Took pity on you in your sopping wet state, I guess. But I know you just want to stop me. You're wasting your time."

"There's a way to do it," he said without preamble. "Verity says you need to modify the chroneon pulse. If I remember right, you can put it between the pulse generator and the emitter to limit the field. Then you can use my ship to send the pulse along the whole history of the rip. Don't you see? You can close the rip without endangering anyone."

"What made you change your mind?"

"I—I didn't. I learned about the add-on. From Verity. She didn't want to tell me. Or you. She still thinks it's too dangerous."

"What's a chroneon pulse?" She put a hand on her hip.

"It's the—what do you call the wave particle generated by the Trigor?"

"A ripeon wave."

"A—really? A ripeon? All right, so a chroneon pulse is a ripeon wave."

"Really. You didn't even know what a ripeon wave was until I just told you."

"Look! It's the pulse that comes out of the thing. For the Instant we called it a chroneon pulse. Whatever you call it, it's the same thing. But the point is, we can design a modulator to tune it, so it works without erasing all of time and space."

Kayla just stared at him, expressionless. She finally raised her eyebrows as if she'd come to a conclusion.

"Show me," she said.

DISCONNECT

"WHY HAS SHE accompanied you?" was all Verity said when Pilot X and Kayla entered the ship.

"I want to show her your modulator idea."

"I think that would be a mistake," Verity said.

"Oh really?" Kayla asked.

"Yes," Verity said evenly. "It could be used as an amplifier as well. And she has stated clearly that she does not mind erasing reality—again—if it saves Koheq."

"Again? I never erased reality," Kayla protested.

"She's not going to erase reality," Pilot X said, as much to convince himself as Verity. "Not after we show her the modulator. Right?" Pilot X asked Kayla directly.

"Why would I?" She shrugged. "If we save Koheq, that's all I care about."

"There's more room in the back. We can use a drafting table back there so Verity can display the whole design. And she will display the whole design," he emphasized. "Come with me." He motioned for Kayla to follow him through the singularity hatch.

She followed him, but he could tell she stopped suddenly. He turned to see why, only to watch her press the manual button to close the hatch, shutting the door between them. Before he could press the button on his side to reopen it, he heard her banging on the door's seal with something.

"STOP NOW!" he heard Verity shout over the speakers. He realized he was jamming the open button, and nothing was happening.

"Verity, reopen the hatch," Pilot X said.

DAMAGE

KAYLA WOKE TO a loud siren blaring. She wondered if there was a fire at the Institute. She noticed the Institute now had metal flooring. She wondered when that got put in. And which lab was she in? Then she remembered. And she panicked.

"Stop it!" she yelled. And the sirens stopped.

"I was trying to wake you," Verity said.

"You electrocuted me."

"I did. You were endangering the ship. You could have broken the ship."

"I didn't?" Kayla was staring at the door that had led to the singularity hatch. It was open and showing the landing yard outside.

"It appears you merely shifted the door hinge a small amount. I believe it is small enough that you can still shift it back into place and reopen the connection." The hatch door slid shut, darkening the cockpit. "I've closed the hatch door, so you can fix what you broke."

"I don't know if I should," Kayla said, still woozy.

"You should," Verity reassured her.

"Or what? You'll shock me again?"

"You need his help."

"I really don't. He just wants to convince me to stop. He's trying to trick me, and I won't let Koheq die."

"He wants to talk to you."

"He can talk to me?"

"Communications are not dependent on the physical connection."

"Kayla," Pilot X said over the intercom. "I want you to let me out of here. But more than that, I need you to trust me. I want to help you save Koheq and not destroy everything. Can you believe me?"

"I suppose I could. I'm not sure I do."

"You can't if you think of it as ending Koheq. You have the unique set of skills to give Koheq a second chance. I didn't have that chance for my people. You—I mean, someone—once told me that my purpose is to tell the story of my universe to yours. To help you not to make the same mistakes we did. Not to let death and destruction reign again. And this time—I can come with you. You can survive. We can fix this. I can fix this. I couldn't take her with me, but I can save you and all your people. You couldn't travel in time then, but now you can." Pilot X was getting confused in his desperation.

"I? Why couldn't I? I've already traveled in time with you."

"I don't mean you. Not exactly. Go to the pilot's chair. Look at the navigation screen."

She did, and there on the screen was a picture of her. But not her. It was her, but her hair was different than she ever remembered having it. And she wore a much different type of clothing. More severe. But on her face was a look of love. She knew without asking that it was a look meant for Pilot X. She felt an unsettling, deep connection with the woman in the picture beyond just the similarity in appearance.

"Who is she?" she asked.

"That's Alexandra," Pilot X said from the other room. "She was a member of something called the Alendan Core. They did not travel in time. They maintained the integrity of the timeline. She convinced me that I had to leave her. Not only leave her but destroy her. Erase her. In order to save everyone else. I wiped her and my entire race out of existence in order to be able to tell you that this universe is better. But I see that it's not better for you. And you are so much like her. And I want to help you, and I can. You just need to let me. The first time I met Alexandra, she gave me a card. A high-quality linen card. I wish I had that card now. That card led to everything. I wish I had a card like that for you now."

"A card? Like this?" Kayla pulled out a linen card. Verity could not read it and Pilot X couldn't see it.

"I don't know. I'd like to see it. Can you let me out?"

Kayla walked over to the hatch. "I just need to move it?"

Verity highlighted an area in laser light on the wall. "If you use your tool to shift it back this much, it should restore function."

Kayla hit the wall. Not hard enough at first. But with Verity's encouragement, she began to see the hatch move a tiny bit. When it lined up with the edge of the laser mark, she stopped.

Verity opened the hatch door. Pilot X was standing there.

Kayla handed him the card. The sturdy linen paper was expensive and had real gold leaf tracery around the edges. Printed in a classic black typeface were the words *Ancient and Respected Order of Koheqi Preservation*, along with an address at the Institute that included a particular office number and invitation code.

"If you would do us the pleasure of meeting with us tonight, I think maybe we would like your advice on something. Come as you will. There will be food," Kayla said.

"Stuffers?" Pilot X said through a few tears.

She laughed. It may have been the first real laugh she'd ever laughed. It was certainly the first Pilot X had seen. "I'll see what we can do."

"What time?" he asked.

"When you arrive." She shrugged. She left the ship slowly this time but without looking back.

"I still don't trust her," said Verity.

"Well, one of us shouldn't. Just to be safe," said Pilot X.

WORK

PILOT X ARRIVED at the location indicated on the card. It was on a tree-lined side street around the corner from where he had entered the Institute when he met with Franciu. An old man sat on a thin metal chair under a red awning. There was no sign, but it gave the impression of being something you only went up to if you already knew what it was.

Pilot X approached the brick building and showed the card. The old man eyeballed it then nodded and slowly stood. He turned toward the door and did something Pilot X couldn't see. The door opened on its own and the man moved out of the way and motioned for Pilot X to enter.

"Do you need the card?" Pilot X asked.

The man just shook his head, so Pilot X pocketed it and entered.

It was dim but not dark inside. The kind of lighting you might find in a nice restaurant that served steak and wine. But it was not a restaurant. Just an empty carpeted hallway with lots of dark wooden doors. The carpet was deep red. The walls were light gray but not institutional. The gray of an old club, not a hospital.

He walked down the hall. One of the doors near the end opened and Kayla came out.

"Thank you for coming," she said as she walked toward Pilot X. He didn't know if he was supposed to shake her hand or hug her. He was certain he shouldn't kiss her, but he had to dismiss the impulse.

"Do you want your card back?" he said, pulling it out of his pocket and showing it to her.

"No. You can keep it. Consider it a memento."

Well, she was different than Alexandra in that respect. Or at least the Respected Order of Koheqi Preservation was different than the Alendan Core had been. He wished he hadn't had to return Alexandra's card. He had nothing of hers to remember her by.

"What is the Respected Order of Koheqi Preservation?" he asked.

"I made it up," she said. "The name just came to me. I was given this wing to operate in. It's an old executive office wing. All the executives from the corporate side of the Institute moved on to extra-stellar operations years ago. They'd been using this for parties and temporary events, but without a big central room, it's not well suited for that. So they gave it to the Order of Retirees. They weren't using it either, so I convinced a few of them to let me at it. A lot of them are old professors of mine, so they said if I did something worthwhile, I could use it for free. So now it's mine. I don't even use most of the rooms except for storage. This one here is my lab."

She opened the door out of which she had arrived, and let Pilot X go in front of her.

The inside of the room contrasted harshly with the sophisticated hallway. It was brightly lit with white tile and steel benches, tables, and chairs. One whole wall had screens showing various scenes, one of which was the door outside. Testing equipment littered the area like someone had stood in the center of the room and spun themselves around while flinging it everywhere. Some of it was on its side or even balanced on a corner.

"Nice place," Pilot X said.

"It's a mess, I know. But nobody ever comes here, so I don't bother keeping it presentable. And I know where everything is."

On one bench, Pilot X recognized what looked like the components of the Instant. The collection of metal devices with cables and nozzles and gauges looked like a jumble if you didn't know they could destroy the universe. He shivered. The differences were subtle, and he would have only been able to tell anyone what they were if he could compare them to a picture. It made his skin crawl at how alike they were.

"You didn't have to set them all up on my account," he said, staring.

She laughed. Again, with the laugh. "I didn't. They were like that. I—heh—I had been planning to activate it yesterday when you interrupted me. I think I'm glad I didn't?" She paused and tilted her head. "Am I? Should I be? Should I trust you?"

"I mean, I think you should," he said. "But you'll just have to let me help you and you see how it goes. I'm kind of at your mercy here. This is your turf. I assume more than just the old man outside would come running if you needed it."

She cocked her head. "That's not what worries me though. I'm worried—I'm not even really worried anymore." She shrugged. "I just wouldn't want it to fail. Even if you didn't mean it to fail, changing the Trigor makes me nervous. I know it will work now. I don't know if it will work after we make your change. I don't know your design like I know mine."

"Let's start there and get you familiar with it."

She took him to another bench and cleared away some testing equipment to reveal a screen they could draw on. He sent designs from Verity to the screen and began walking through them. She didn't really need him there for this. She anticipated everything he did. When he paused to remember a particular function or reason for a connection, she would guess what it was. By the end, she was excited and smiling and understanding, and he felt like she had shown him the designs, not the other way around.

"You're smart," he said.

"I am. But you are too. You just—you just pause sometimes."

"Side effects," he said.

She nodded. "Of the Trig—or your thing."

"The Instant."

MODIFICATIONS

KAYLA KNEW HER way around a soldering iron and circuits. Pilot X just stepped back and tried to help where he could. The add-on should rightly have taken a few weeks to put together, but Kayla already had a lot of the components they needed. Plus, she was a genius at seeing quicker ways to do things without sacrificing quality. And she was just good. Pilot X kept asking questions that turned out to be irrelevant.

"It's going to take a while to harden the T-board," he'd say for example. "I'll get started on that."

"Oh wait," Kayla would respond. "I have my own method. Just use the minikiln over there on the P setting and pouch it with a couple of loose doses and it will finish in, like, an eighth of the time."

"Loose doses?"

"Yeah, like this." And she'd do something highly irregular, like open some capsules of dosing material and just sprinkle them on the board.

"That works?"

"It works!" she'd say enthusiastically. And she was right.

Or he would start laying down a few custom circuits only to have her lean over his shoulder and say, "You know I use a projection sprayer for stuff like that. You can basically insta-etch them. Here, let me show you."

They took few breaks, but when they did, they ate what little food was around and talked.

"No," Kayla said, "for the hundredth time, all I have are lilke bars and caffeinated lemon soda. If you want coffee, you're going to have to leave."

He almost did. But he didn't want to lose any time. Or let her out of his sight. He sniffed at the lemon soda. "This is what you drink?" he said.

She lifted a paper cup. "Finest kind!" she said. "My dad used to say that. From some old vid or other, I suppose. That's all he would do in the evening when I was a kid, watch videos."

"You haven't been my Helvy since you joined Rorger's gang," Pilot X said.

"How does an alien from another timeline know the *Koheq Gang*?" Kayla laughed. "My dad *loved* that one. Wore it out."

"Is he still around?" Pilot X risked asking.

She shook her head, and changed the subject. "You talk to yourself when you work."

"Do I? I hadn't noticed."

"Verity never told you?"

"Verity hasn't seen me work much lately. I have two modes. Wallowing, and avoiding my feelings by tracking down a woman who is accidentally about to destroy the world."

She put down her drink and gave him a stern look.

"I'm sorry," he said in a rush. "It was a joke."

"No, it's OK. It's just—"

"Just what?"

"You do."

"Do what?"

"Hide. You're always running. I guess I just noticed it. Even when you're here with me working, you're running from something."

He tried to laugh but it came out as a choke. "Yeah," was all he could manage. If it had been the Matriarch or Lal or even Prishat, he would have just brushed it off with a denial and a joke. But Kayla's blue eyes had locked onto him and he couldn't move. Couldn't dodge. Couldn't make his usual play for a grand gesture or glib comment. She saw him. And he couldn't get away.

"It's why I'm here," he finally said. "I've been running away from this"—he motioned to the parts of the Trigor—"and toward it at the same time. It's enough . . ." He laughed without any joy. "It's enough to drive you mad a little bit." He looked down and smiled a smile he knew must have looked insane. But when he looked up, she was right there by him.

She put a hand on his shoulder. "I know. And you can fix this."

He smiled back. Then he took a swig of the lemon soda. "I—cannot stand one more sip of this. Let's get back to work and fix your stellar system fast so I never have to drink that again."

They worked and took a break for bad jokes about lemon soda and choked down bars a few more times, but the conversations stayed lighter after that. With this rhythm, they packed in ten to twelve days of work into a night and most of the next day. In the end, they had a working add-on.

"OK, let's use this electrogen to send a test pulse through. It's not ripeons or—what did you call them? Chroneons? But it will make sure the paths are right and they can attenuate."

Pilot X hooked up the system for the test. He had learned basic electronic test sequences in flight school. It was something he could do without worrying that he was taking six times as long as Kayla.

"All set. Let her rip," he said.

Kayla turned it on from her end and the lights on the testing rig all glowed green. Then something began to smoke. Then it caught fire. Then both of them were scrambling to put out the fire. Then they were leaning against the table splattered in foam and trying to catch their breath without breathing in too much smoke.

"What happened?" Kayla said.

Pilot X reviewed everything. There was a burn mark at a junction leading in from where the chroneon pulse would first enter the modulator. They had a used a cheap type of resistor there, and Pilot X just realized that while it was fine to handle a low-voltage pulse, the electric one they had just sent through was a touch too powerful.

"That resistor can't take electricity," they both said at once.

"Well, at least I wasn't behind you on this one." Pilot X laughed.

"I think we had the path all right," she said, squinting at the assembly as if she could re-create the test before it went bad.

"We can't think. We have to be sure," Pilot X said. "We need to test it again. And I don't think a lower voltage will be enough. We need actual chroneons."

"You know, we have a ripeon generator right here," she said, forgetting to call them chroneons, and pointing at the Trigor.

"I just said we have to be sure—"

"No, we just disassemble the amplifier portion. It'll send a low-spectrum pulse without the effect."

"I hate adding that much uncertainty to the whole thing."

"I can test the entire Trigor without—"

"No. No more test pulses. That's what drew me here in the first place. You were playing with fire then and we're still playing with fire if we do it now."

She raised her voice. "So this was your plan? To get us to an impasse and insist we can't go any further?!"

"Hold on a minute. I said I didn't like disassembling things and putting them back together. Adds more opportunities for things to go wrong. I didn't say we couldn't do it. It's just—well, is it our only option?"

"No," she said with a sharp shake of the head. "Putting it in the full Trigor at low pulse is the other option. But since you don't want to do that, then that's your other option." She slammed down a pack of new resistors she was holding.

"Hey! This is going to be fine."

"No, it's not going to be fine, Pilot X. It's not going to be fine unless it's perfect and right now it's not perfect and it's not clear we can make it perfect because our clear path just got muddied." She was crying just a little bit.

Pilot X realized he was crying a bit too. "What if we get Verity to validate the test?"

"She hates me. She'll just say it isn't valid," Kayla sputtered.

"She doesn't hate you and she can't lie."

"You just caught her lying," she said.

"Well, she finds it really hard to lie. And that wasn't a lie of commission; it was a lie of omission."

"Makes me feel so much better," Kayla grumbled.

"Let's take off the chroneon amp and try the path. Step by step."

They took their time to remove the amplifier and reattach the add-on. While doing it, Kayla had three more revelations that helped them reattach everything faster.

"I think even with having to take the amp off, this actually is easier than trying to add the modifier in to the whole Trigor. Wish I'd thought of this earlier."

With a new resistor in place and the amplifier attached, Pilot X got the test ready a second time.

"All set," he said. They flipped the switch.

Nothing happened. Which was good. All the test lights were green.

"And we're still here." Kayla smirked. "We didn't kill the timeline."

"It's true, Pat. This here Eliminator device seems to be working fine. I bet we can save the Pineapple Planet."

"Ha. Ha. Ha," Kayla said, clearly emphasizing each *ha*. "Next you'll tell me the Pineapple Planet is real."

Pilot X opened his mouth and then shut it quickly. When he opened it again, he almost immediately wished he had shut it a second time. "I still think we should have Verity validate it."

"Of course you do! Why not scoop up everything half assembled and cart it halfway across the circle so your pet spaceship can tell us we're wrong?"

"Kayla—"

"Fine! Help me get it in the backpack."

"Backpack?"

"Yeah, it's an easy way to carry stuff that straps on your back."

"I know what a backpack is."

"What's the problem then?"

"This is not going to all fit in a backpack." He pointed to the several rather large pieces of the Trigor, one of which had a somewhat bulky growth on it that was the new add-on.

"You haven't seen my backpack," she said.

He had not seen anything like it before. It was almost as tall as him but came with gravity actuators on the frame that aligned in a sort of upside-down pyramid on the back.

"It sends the weight into the ground as weightons."

"Weightons? You mean gravitons?"

"I actually mean gravitons. But it's starting to entertain me to come up with ridiculous words for things and see if I can get you to accept them as real Koheqi terms. Don't look at me like that. I'm the one who has to deal with your jealous spaceship."

"It's not a spaceship," was all he could manage to say.

"Oh?" she said, adjusting the gargantuan backpack.

"It's a timeship."

"Well, whatever it is, take me to it."

"You're not going to fall over with that thing on?"

"No. Stop doubting me. Onward, timeshipper," she said. "That's what we call people who fly timeships on Koheq."

"It absolutely is not," he said.

"It is now. We never had timeships before. I just decided you're a timeshipper, timeshipper. Get used to it."

The old man outside had been replaced by a somewhat older man who was no more talkative than the previous one. He didn't blink an eye at Kayla's backpack, merely holding the door open until they were both out, then settling back down into his chair.

"If nobody uses this hall, why do superfluous old men agree to guard it for you?" Pilot X asked.

"Those are not superfluous old men. Those are professors of the Order of Retirees, and they volunteer to watch the door for me. It's a long story. Suffice to say, they were all great teachers and I was a great student."

Pilot X shrugged. "They seem awful quiet for professors," he said.

"They're studying. Implants." She tapped her temple.

"Oh, of course. Side effects," he said, tapping his own temple.

TESTING

WITH HER BACKPACK, Kayla raised more than a few eyebrows on the shuttle, but they made it to the landing lot without incident. Verity agreed without much protest or even veiled AI snarkiness to verify the test.

"Let's set it up in the cockpit, not the storage singularity," Pilot X said. "That way we can finish it in here, where we'll need it when we activate it."

He felt the chill run through him when he said the word *activate*. As much as he told himself they were doing the right thing, part of him still opposed ever taking that action again.

It was crowded in the small floor area in front of the passenger chairs, but they got it done. Verity said nothing as they worked, which either meant they were doing it right or she was really mad. It was probably both.

"All set," Pilot X said. "Ready for validation test. Verity, are you ready?"

"I'm in observation mode and ready for the test," she said.

He flipped the switch and the lights went green. Everything went the same as before.

"Validation fail," said Verity.

"Here we go," said Kayla, throwing up her hands.

"What happened?" said Pilot X.

"Initial chroneon volume is under bound," Verity said.

Pilot X sighed. "Well, you could have told us that before we started."

"I was unsure if you meant to adjust the amount."

"During the test?"

"Yes, during the test," Verity said.

So much for avoiding AI snarkiness.

"Verity, what should the test chroneon volume be?"

"Fifteen hundred," Verity said.

"What? No! That'll blow the resistor," Kayla protested.

"Verity, even the Instant only ran at eight hundred. We're going to modulate this quite a bit below that."

"Fifteen hundred would be a standard stress test."

Pilot X looked at Kayla and shook his head. "Fine, setting at fifteen hundred."

"It'll blow the resistor," Kayla said again, shaking her head, but set up for a second test.

When everyone was ready, Pilot X flipped the switch again. Lights went green. One went red.

Pilot X stared at the spot where the resistor was. It was holding. "Verity?"

She was taking longer than she needed to.

"Validated," she said. Pilot X turned it off.

"However," Verity said.

"What now?" Kayla yelled.

"You had a red indicator light on your test machine. You should troubleshoot that before proceeding."

"That's the 1K warning indicator letting us know we were exceeding chroneon tolerances," Pilot X said, smiling. "But we knew that because you set the test above 1K at fifteen hundred, remember? So we can dismiss that warning."

"Ah," was all Verity said.

OBJECTIONS

THIS CLOSE TO the rift, space felt different to Pilot X. He suspected it was mostly in his head. There was an observable black streak where the rift affected space and blocked light from coming in from behind it, but if you didn't know it was there, and you weren't an astronomer, you'd dismiss it as an arbitrary dark patch in the sky.

Verity hadn't said much since they'd left Koheq.

"We need to calculate a safe point as late in the timeline as possible near the rift," he said.

At first Kayla thought he was talking to her and opened her mouth to answer, but Verity beat her to it.

"The rift reaches a natural limit approximately 554,327 Koheqi orbits from now. Orbits are mostly virtual projections, as Koheq stops orbiting eventually."

It felt a little like rubbing salt in Kayla's wound, but Pilot X ignored it. "Shift us there."

Verity said nothing, but the ship shuddered and moved.

Now the rift was obvious. A large portion of the view was empty and there was a thin glow of radiation around its rim. There wasn't a star. There wasn't even debris from the stellar system anymore. But this was as large as it would get. It was not a universe-threatening anomaly. This was only about Koheq. Which brought up another issue.

"Verity? Where do we do this?"

When he had activated the Instant, he had landed on a moon near a battle. The battle allowed him to easily register the signatures of the three warring civilizations that would be removed from history. Other than that, it didn't really matter where he had put it, since it was meant to affect the entire universe.

Now they only wanted to remove the rift from history and that, ideally, would only affect the rift. They wanted to make sure that was the case. There was no undo button on the Instant. Or the Trigor.

"The device can be activated from within the ship. That will protect us. If modulated properly, its effective radius will only apply to the rift," Kayla said too casually. Kayla got to work calibrating the device to that end. It was a calculation that had to be right.

"Check this," she said, showing her math on a screen. Pilot X checked it, but he was doubtful he would find an error. He was doubtful that if an error were there that he would see it. Pilots had to be good at math but—side effects.

"It looks right." He hesitated but asked her: "Verity?"

"The calculations do not appear to have an error. I must take this opportunity to warn you once again that we cannot be certain this will work as you expect. Your first test revealed a transistor fault that, while unlikely, could still happen with the chroneon pulse. Your most recent test with chroneons was nonstandard and also resulted in an error light. This may, as you pointed out, be due to signal limits in the test, but that cannot be determined with required certainty on one test. This is an irresponsible and risky attempt to solve a problem that is personal by nature and ill-advised. The only thing in its favor is that we will remain unaffected. But given the emotional effect the Instant had on you, it is also undetermined what effect any mistakes with the Trigor would have on both of you if you accidentally caused damage to the Koheqi or any other civilization because of an error, however improbable."

Even Kayla didn't protest, for once.

"Consider it this way," Verity continued. "If you do nothing, all Koheqi that you know will survive and, as we discovered, the civilization will move on. If you do nothing, Koheqi life will continue. If you proceed, you have a chance of eliminating it. A very small chance, yes, but a chance. Is the location of future Koheqi, which you do not know, worth the risk of destroying everything?"

This hit home with Pilot X. He had done just that to save the universe. It felt like the same decision in miniature. He turned to Kayla.

"Verity may be exaggerating the chances, but she's right. It is a chance. We have to acknowledge the risk here. You once—I mean—Alexandra once convinced me that the universe was more important than my own civilization. This is your civilization. Only you can make this decision, and you've heard all the arguments. I believe we can do this, but she's not wrong. It's a risk. Do you want to take that risk? Do you want to take on that burden on behalf of your people?"

"We should ask them," Kayla said.

"Ask them?" Verity said.

"Yes," continued Kayla. "Verity, can you take us to a point where the Koheqi are making the decision to leave Koheq?"

"It is not a single point in time. It was an action taken slowly over a long period of time."

"But you can determine the point of greatest importance, the point when the decision became inevitable?"

Verity took a long time to respond. "I could."

"Will you?"

"I—I—"

Pilot X had never heard Verity stutter before. "Verity?"

"I will follow pilot instructions," she said, quoting a basic directive, something she rarely did anymore.

Pilot X didn't hesitate. "If you can take us to just before that point, do it."

The shudder was almost immediate. Koheq popped back into view.

"Now what?" Pilot X asked.

"I'm going to ask." Kayla shrugged.

"That's interfering in the timeline," he said.

Kayla rubbed her chin. "Not if we do it right."

QUESTION

KAYLA'S PLAN WAS ridiculous. She wanted Pilot X to present himself to the Institute of Psychology of this era as an anthropologist studying the Koheqi migration. She tried to give him everything else he would need to know.

"Isn't your knowledge outdated at this point in time?" he asked her.

"Maybe," she said in a casual way. "But I've noticed three things that give me confidence in this plan. One, the Institute rarely changes its nature over centuries. Two, you are really good at making friends. And three, you are much more successful when you do what I tell you."

Kayla proved much better than Glonda or Franciu at navigating the politics of Institute audiences. Her knowledge may have been old, but it seemed to work even better because of that.

Pilot X stood at the counter in the office of visiting academics, waiting for Lola to finish whatever it was she was doing. Lola was dressed all in black, with her shoulders, arms, and head bare except for immense circular gold earrings. She tapped out a few last things on her screen, which Pilot X assumed must have finished off his application or verification or whatever it was they had done this time. He'd had so many of these bureaucratic appointments, he had lost track.

"Well, this all seems to be in order." She leaned toward him, letting her gold earrings almost touch the desk in front of her. "I must say, sir"—she looked around as if someone in the otherwise empty office might hear her—"it's nice to see someone who knows how to adhere to the proper forms of tradition, unlike the young folk these days." She smiled widely at the compliment she believed she had just given him. He just now noticed her lipstick was purple. "And you, not even a Koheqi." She tapped the desk as she laughed at her—joke?

"Lola, you're a dear. I don't know what I would have done without you."

"Nonsense," she said, turning her head. "You made it easy." She tapped a few more things on her screen, making Pilot X fear she was beginning another long document, but she looked up almost immediately. "Department Head Matra of Koheqi World Mentality will meet you at a particularly lovely diner near the Institute of Psychology. The address and other details are all in the message I just sent. She's so excited to meet you!"

"Go!" Kayla said. You need to be there on time. Don't forget to review the identity details we made for you. You need to get this right." She had drilled him on the identity all night last night. He knew it was important.

"I just need to finish my coffee!" he complained.

"They have coffee there. It's a diner. You don't want to make this department head wait for you and lose her excitement."

"Why is this person so excited to meet me, anyway?" he said, finally getting up to go.

Neither Verity nor Kayla answered. That was suspicious.

"What?" he said to the room.

"I may have asked Verity to plant some stories about you in the Koheqi media," she said.

"I knew I felt shudders," he muttered. "Anything I should know about myself?"

"It's all in the identity we practiced. Just stick to that and stay humble," she said, patting him on the back. "Which, I just realized, we should have practiced. But do your best."

Professor Matra insisted on paying for the coffee and berry stuffers. The berries were in season and amazing.

"I was thrilled to get your call," she said, smoothing down her sensible, light brown business attire. "I'm a little embarrassed to say I'm a big fan. I've been following the stories. What you did on Pantoon. Well. Impressive." She smiled a shy smile and pressed her long, thin hands against the table before raising them to check that her black hair was still pulled into a knot at the back of her head. It was. She smiled again but kept her dark black eyes firmly looking at Pilot X.

He really wished he had been told what he supposedly did on Pantoon. He just nodded and smiled humbly. "Well, thank you. That's very kind of you to say. But I'm here to talk about Koheq."

"Yes! Migration psychology is, as you might imagine, a hot topic right now."

Pilot X described Kayla's plan for a worldwide survey to determine attitudes toward migration, including attitudes toward theoretical ways—well, one way—that migration could be avoided.

"Now, this is the sticking point, but it is essential to my research," he said. "We don't want to raise hopes. We understand there is no other way forward. But we need to understand the mind-set. I need to ask people, *if* there were a way to save Koheq, but there was a small risk that the way could result in Koheq being destroyed, would they be in favor of pursuing it anyway?"

Matra frowned a little. "Yes, that is sticky. We've done a lot to convince people there is no other way forward and yet we still have conspiracy theorists who say a way is hidden. And, well, to put it bluntly, their conspiracy theory matches your question. I mean. Is there any other way to get at the data you want? It's a bit of a nonstarter." She looked upset that she might have to disappoint Pilot X.

He expected this. "There's no other way than that question. It's been highly crafted. But I believe, and I'd like you to attempt to confirm for yourself, that if presented properly—even at the expense of other questions—this could actually lay to rest the conspiracy theory itself. It might be the best defense against it."

Matra leaned back in her chair. "It would have to be the only question we asked for that to work. I can't imagine—"

"That would be fine," he said. "As long as demographic questions are also allowed." He didn't care about demographic questions, but Kayla had emphasized that getting rid of demo questions would be suspicious.

Matra waved her hand, not even looking at Pilot X anymore. "Of course, demo questions are assumed. I—well, if you're willing to go that far, I think we could do it. I know how I'd present it. We even discussed something similar before—but coming from the Institute, it didn't project to work. Coming from a celebrity anthropologist—well, simply put—that makes all the difference." She smiled and met his gaze again.

"And if people answer that it's worth the risk?" he asked. He didn't want to ask this, but Kayla had insisted.

"It gives us the opportunity to call for proposals again and when none come, which they won't, it puts it to bed for good," she said, smiling. She smiled a bit too much for someone talking about manipulating the psychology of a whole planet that knew it was going to be destroyed.

THE VOTE

KOHEQ WAS ADVANCED enough at this point that a secure worldwide poll did not take long. The setup, explanation, and required public conversation and comment period took all the time. Pilot X had to appear in public with the Institute's luminaries to explain his study. Everywhere he went, people cheered and swamped him for autographs.

Verity had outdone herself in tightbeam time broadcasts.

"I spent some time when you were wallowing in the hut going over media simulation. It allowed me to exercise otherwise unused pathways," she said when he asked her about it. "I am very pleased with the work."

The night of the vote, Matra expected Pilot X to join her as the results came in. He wanted Kayla there too, but she said it was too risky, since they hadn't planted a cover story for her.

"We could just say you're my assistant?" he said.

"No, we couldn't. I'll watch from here with Verity."

Verity said nothing.

The results would take about a day to tabulate. Each citizen who wished to vote would cast their vote within a few hours of sunrise. This meant that results would not be complete until one full rotation of Koheq. The tallies would not be updated publicly until all votes were in, but Pilot X would be allowed to see them in real time.

Verity would monitor through Pilot X's wrist device and relay the information to Kayla.

The early time zones voted heavily against. These were Institute-heavy areas, partly because the Institute of Psychology, as the vote's sponsor, set it to begin with its own sunrise. As the day rolled on, the percentage moved slowly toward 50–50—very slowly—and then began to drift apart again. By the time there were only two time zones left, the vote stood at 68 percent against taking the theoretical action. Matra took this as an excellent sign of the Institute's effectiveness in getting people to face the reality of migration.

The last two time zones were not similar to each other in any way. The first zone contained a long, thin continent that stretched almost from pole to pole and held some of the most abundant agricultural land in Koheq. It was expected they would vote heavily for taking the risk, since they had been the most vocal against migration in the early days and the idea of some way out still appealed to them, even if only theoretical.

The last time zone was made up mostly of heavily urbanized and highly populated islands. Each island had its own Institute, usually involved in some way with advanced technologies. These were expected to dismiss the idea and vote against taking the risk, even if theoretical.

The votes from the "farm zone," as Matra kept calling it, narrowed the percentage to 58 percent against. The vote in the zone itself was well above 90 percent for taking the risk; it just didn't have a large population.

"That won't be enough," Matra said. "But it's good to know. We still have a little work to do in the farm zone."

The first tallies from the Urban Islands began to arrive. The 58 went from 59 to 60 percent against, and the room began to relax. Pilot X felt for Kayla. Kayla hadn't necessarily committed to being bound by the vote, but she wouldn't have gone to all this trouble if she didn't intend to respect it.

The early tallies were small in the Urban Islands. People made jokes about tech workers sleeping in. Everyone expected the results to be uniform. They were engaging in a form of the recency bias, imagining the early votes were some kind of representative sample. As the tallies began to speed up, it appeared that, fallacy or no, it would hold true. The 60 went back to 59, then back to 60, hovering around what would appear to be the end mark.

Then votes from two islands known for "soft technologies" started flooding in. Pilot X never got a precise definition of *soft technologies*. It involved software but also some hardware. One person referred to refrigerator magnets or something. Pilot X couldn't be sure.

Whatever soft technologies were, they apparently involved iconoclastic beliefs: 58 became 57, then 56. People in the room rolled their eyes. The "softies" were unpredictable. They should have seen this coming. Population-wise, they weren't enough to swing it back the other way, but they might make it close.

And then it happened. A late surge of votes in islands from earlier in the time zone came in too. The late risers apparently wished for a way out of migration: 56 became 55, then 53, then 50, then 49, then 50 percent against, then 48. The room went silent and tense. They couldn't believe it. The final tally ended up with 51.1 percent in favor of taking the risk. Pilot X could not keep the smile from his face.

"You're smiling," Matra said, shocked.

Pilot X shook his head. "I'm sorry. It's not over the outcome; it's over the data flow. It's fascinating." He wasn't lying about it being fascinating. He was only lying about why he smiled.

Verity landed, and Pilot X boarded.

"Well." He smiled, his arms wide. "We have an answer."

Kayla was grinning as well. Pilot X imagined Verity frowning and her tone of voice didn't betray it, but her choice of words did.

"It is still true that almost half of Koheq does not believe it is worth the risk."

"Verity, come on—" Pilot X said.

"No, it's all right," Kayla interrupted. "Verity, you're right. But we should also keep in mind that this is a theoretical possibility. Many people may have voted against it because it's not real to them and they have just been subjected to a long campaign to convince them to make their peace with migration."

"It's also possible people voted for it because of the lack of a real risk," Verity said.

"Yes, that's true, but the campaign implies the population leaned the way I describe."

"That—is fair," Verity said.

"Well, that's as good as unanimity in my book," Pilot X said. "Verity, take us back to the end point of the rift."

The shimmer was not immediate. But it came.

RISK

THE TRIGOR WAS partly assembled. The chroneon generator and the modulator were in one part. The rest of the device was in another. Verity insisted on one more test at a low-chroneon level that would not set off the red warning light. Pilot X took this as a good sign.

"She wants to have all greens. It's an obsessive-compulsive thing for AIs."

"I can hear you," Verity said.

"I never thought otherwise," Pilot X said.

The test at eight hundred worked fine. All greens. Kayla silently attached the rest of the Trigor. She looked up at Pilot X as she made the last connection. He decided to make a speech.

"We stand on the brink of a great moment—" he started.

"There is no need to make a speech," Verity interrupted. "We are ready to proceed."

"Just let me have this moment," Pilot X said.

"Must we?" Verity asked.

"I think we should let him have it," said Kayla.

Verity said nothing.

"I just mean, this is it. This is a moment we'll never get back. We are living right now, this very moment, in the way things were. After we flick that switch, we will not be able to go back here. Maybe that seems obvious to you, but it's been one of the hardest things to get used to. Growing up, I assumed that any instant could be revisited. Not changed, of course, but revisited. Even if you weren't a timeship operator or passenger, all Alendans assumed that someone could go to any point in space-time.

"After the Instant, I couldn't. All the moments of my life and the entire universe were gone. Overwritten. I can't go back to the moment I flicked the switch. It's forever out of my reach. Sometimes I think there must be some dimension in which it still exists, but that's my Alendan upbringing. We were taught that time was like a titanium cube. You could travel around inside it, but changing it was almost impossible. But I changed it. And that is irrevocable. I know that now. I've lived it.

"What we're about to do is just as irrevocable, even if it's on a smaller scale. But it will have effects, especially on the latter history of Koheq. And that's something we can't take back. Kayla, I know you're doing this to save people. But one last time, remember, you're changing the lives of every person who left Koheq. You're changing their existence. And there may be people who do not exist anymore because of your actions. The people who go to Gravell and Bentria will no longer need to go there. Are you sure?"

"Yes." She nodded solemnly and reached for the switch.

"No." Pilot X stopped her hand. "I've done this before. I can take the burden."

She gently removed his hand from hers. "No." She shook her head. "This is my burden. Verity? Are we in place?"

"Yes," Verity said. Pilot X waited for a snarky rejoinder or added comment, but Verity stayed quiet.

"For Koheq," Kayla whispered, and flipped the switch.

Pilot X was stunned. When he'd switched on the Instant, the changes were subtle. The war disappeared from the sky, but the ground stayed the same. This time everything changed. The ship bucked and kicked as an entire stellar system emerged around them. The ship felt out of control, like it was rolling.

"Verity?"

"The ship is caught in several intersecting gravity currents. It was not possible to predict where the system would return. Priority was given to position for activation of the Trigor."

"And?" Pilot X encouraged her to tell him she was about to get things under control and stabilize the ship.

"I cannot regain control or stabilize the ship."

"Unidentified vessel, this is Koheq Stellar Command, do you require assistance?" a voice boomed through the speakers.

"It worked!" Kayla smiled, her eyes bright amid the chaos.

"Maybe too well," Pilot X said. "Can you ask for help?"

"Koheq Stellar Command, this is Verity. We have jumped to this point unexpectedly and were caught in tempor—in gravitational shears." Verity caught herself before revealing they were a timeship.

"Jumped from where, Verity? We didn't see you before you—never mind. Transferring you to the KSC ship *Kayla*. They're the nearest to you."

Pilot X and Kayla gave each other a look.

"Coincidence, right?" Kayla said.

Pilot X shrugged.

"Verity, this is the *Calla*." Pilot X and Kayla shared a look. Bad pronunciation? "Verity, we'd like to get you out of there, but you're in a pickle," *Calla*'s officer said.

"Calla, who am I speaking with?" Verity asked.

"This is Captain Hab, and who am I speaking with?"

"My name is Verity. I'll explain that later. Our pilot is Pilot X. Please define *pickle*."

"Oh, you're the ship's AI," Captain Hab said. "No need to explain. I get it. Is Pilot X incapacitated or hurt?"

"Negative, Pilot X is fine," Verity said. "As is our only other passenger."

"Got it. Well, give the pilot my regards."

"Captain Hab sends his regards to you—"

"I heard," Pilot X said. "Find out about the pickle."

"Captain Hab, please define *pickle.*"

"Oh right. Well, a pickle is a sort of toroid-shaped gravity shear. It only occurs in a few well-plotted places. It's an oddity of this system. They come and go as the planets and moons move, and they're normally very easy to avoid. I'm—curious—how you managed not to miss this one."

"Thank you, Captain. I understand now, and I have plotted the shape you describe. There does not seem—"

Verity cut out as the ship began to topple forward and back with more violence.

"Come again, Verity," Captain Hab said.

"I am unable to plot a safe entry point to the . . . pickle for you to render aid."

"Well, that's just it—"

The ship was tossed, and a few panels began to smoke under the stress of the shear. Some smaller screens went dead. If they lost Verity, they'd be done for. But Pilot X let her continue the conversation. She could think faster than he could. Especially these days.

"—or we'd just lift you out," Captain Hab's voice returned. The ship rocked hard to port and began to vibrate. It was not pleasant.

"We missed most of that, Captain Hab, but I surmise you explained that the pickle is dangerous for you to enter and difficult for us to exit."

"That's the long and short of it," Captain Hab said. "I can come alongside near you and try to poke my nose in. Maybe we can hook you or—"

"The danger to your ship and crew is too high; I cannot advise you render aid in that fashion."

"Well, I don't know how else to render it. You'll either get pulled apart by the torsion soon or it will pop you out like a cork. Those are essentially the only options."

"Thank you, Captain. We'll consider these options." Verity paused. "I have communicated with the vessel. We are unable to receive aid from them without endangering their ship. I have advised them not to interfere."

"Yes, we heard," Pilot X said. "Well, what do we do next, then?"

"We will most likely get torn apart by the gravitational forces." The vibrating stopped, but the ship began to get thrown side to side with frequent shudders punctuating the end of each swing. Kayla looked fine, just smiling. Pilot X felt like puking. Verity continued. "The smallest possibility is that we will be thrown from the shear, but in that case, we may be so damaged that we will crash into the abandoned observation station around the nearest moon and be destroyed."

"And you are all right with that?" Pilot X yelled.

"It really worked," Kayla said, ignoring them both.

"All other actions we could take would lead to quicker destruction at this point."

Pilot X threw up. The ship was spinning like a top, and loose bits were beginning to fly around the compartment and occasionally hit him in the temple. That really made it difficult to concentrate on coming up with impossible plans that would save their lives.

"Structural failure shortly," Verity said, not helping.

"Could use more precise measurements right about now," Pilot X complained.

"Verity, time-jump us back to my time," Kayla said.

"Oh," Verity said, and then there was a shimmer.

The buffeting stopped, and the ship stabilized.

"Ship stabilized," Verity said.

"Verity, did Kayla just outthink you?" Pilot X teased.

"No," Verity said.

"But if I'm not mistaken, she thought to do a time jump and you hadn't thought of that."

"I had considered it," Verity said, sounding not at all defensive. "It was too dangerous to attempt until the timing of Kayla's command, when I was forced in response to recheck."

"So Kayla made you recheck."

"Yes."

"So she thought of something you didn't."

"I would not characterize it that way."

"Well, however you characterize it, I'm just glad it worked," Kayla put in.

They were in orbit above Koheq just after the time point they had left for the future.

"Let's see how it worked," Pilot X said. "Verity, take us down."

CHANGES

THE LANDING LOT looked the same.

"I think these are the same ships that were parked here when we left," Pilot X said.

"They are. With one exception. The freighter ship *MaryAnn* is labeled *MaryAnne* with an *e* at the end."

"Well, that's not a good sign," Pilot X joked.

"It's not?" Kayla said, looking worried.

Pilot X realized he shouldn't toy with her emotions just now. "Sorry. It's probably nothing. The fact that a thing has changed is not concerning at all. We knew things would change forward in time from your perspective, right? The whole point was to change things so the system wasn't destroyed. That it may have had past consequences is to be expected too, and those past consequences should be minimal."

"Like *Anne* being spelled with an *e*," Kayla said, reassuring herself.

"Exactly."

"I'll tell you what my test is going to be," Pilot X said.

"What's that?" Kayla said.

"Do stuffers taste the same? I may need to eat several to be sure."

"Oh, you mean pie?" she said innocently.

Pilot X held up a finger, laughing. "Oh no, you don't. You weren't affected."

Kayla laughed. "You're right. I could not call stuffers 'pie' with a straight face." She got serious. "Oh. I hope that didn't really happen. I'll never be able to order one again."

The shuttle looked the same. The people on the shuttle looked generally the same. The signs on the shuttle were different. But wouldn't they be? Most of them were ads anyway. They could have changed them out that morning and it wouldn't mean anything had happened to the timeline.

Pilot X let out a sigh of relief as they neared the café. Down the street was the bar and inside the café, Glonda was behind the counter. She looked out the window at the two of them but made no sign she recognized them.

"Well, here goes. Let's find out if we ever visited here and if you still exist." Pilot X took a deep breath.

"No pressure." Kayla exhaled. They opened the door. As they walked up to the counter, Glonda raised her head from something she had been writing.

"Can I help you?" She smirked.

"Do you remember me?" Pilot X asked.

Glonda scratched her head. "Uh, hmmm. Gee, I don't know."

Kayla let out a gasp. "What about me?"

"Little miss pushy with her stuffers. You, I remember."

"Oh no, we wiped you out of the timeline, Pilot X!" Kayla said.

"Oh no, Aches. You've been wiped out of the timeline," Glonda said in mock drama. "Now you owe me another pineapple stuffer because I can't remember the first one you made me bake."

Pilot X sighed. "We're fine, Kayla."

Kayla slammed her hand down on the counter. "Not funny!"

"Not for someone without a sense of humor," Glonda shot back.

"Dear friends? Must we fight?" Pilot X interceded.

Glonda sighed and stuck out her hand to Kayla. "I'm sorry. I blame my brother. He made me this way."

Kayla looked skeptical but shook Glonda's hand. "I'm sorry too."

Glonda nodded.

"How is Lamar?" Pilot X asked.

"Since you saw him yesterday? I wouldn't know. I haven't seen him since then either."

"Was it just yesterday?"

"Uh, yeah. What is with you two? Are you drunk on breek?"

All of this was making Pilot X feel very good.

"No, but we messed with some dark forces that might have changed history," he answered. "So it's good to hear that not only do you remember us, but that your brother is Lamar and people still drink breek." Pilot X laughed.

"I shouldn't joke that Lamar doesn't drink anymore, should I?" Glonda asked.

"No. You should not. But I'll tell you what you should do! Get us two coffees and two cherry stuffers please!" He grinned a grin as wide as the relief he felt.

"Coming right up!" Glonda busied herself getting the food and drinks.

"It looks like we did it?" Kayla asked.

"Yes, it does. We may want to breeze through some historical records so you can tell me if you see anything alarming like the first president of Koheq was a puppy or something, but it looks as if everything is on track."

Kayla half closed her eyes and smiled. "It feels good."

"Two cherry stuffers and two teas," Glonda said.

"And you still work on the weird visitor credit system, right?" Pilot X asked, picking up his plate and mug.

"Well, I wouldn't call it weird, but yes. It hasn't changed since yesterday," Glonda said.

Pilot X took a big sip of his mug and almost spit it back out. "What is this?"

"Tea," Glonda said.

"Stop joking around, Glonda. I ordered coffee."

"Now I wish I hadn't joked so much," Glonda said. "Because you're not going to believe me. I'm the girl who cried Gorn. But—I thought you said something weird. Then I thought I must have misheard and what you said ended in *e* and I know you drink tea every time you come in here, so I just assumed I misheard and I got you tea . . ." She trailed off.

"Oh no," Kayla said.

"No, I said *coffee*," Pilot X.

"Oh, dear me, no," Kayla said.

"What's coffee?" Glonda asked.

"Hot black liquid brewed up and tasting like heaven?" Pilot X said.

"Yeah. Tea. I don't know what weird word you call it where you're from, but we call that tea."

"No. No," Pilot X protested.

"This isn't happening." Kayla put her hands on her head and stared at Pilot X, who was not smiling, even in his eyes.

"Tea is hot, light brown liquid made from leaves that's passable as a drink at certain times, I'll admit. But coffee. Is a thing. That I have had in this very café. It's hot, black, and brewed from ground beans and it is the stuff of life itself."

"Brewed from beans?" Glonda said, looking disgusted. "Like you eat with rice? Sounds disgusting."

"We wiped out coffee," Kayla said.

"Don't even say that." Pilot X held his hand out in front of him as if warding off a blow.

"So, you know what coffee is?" Glonda asked Kayla.

"Yeah," she admitted. "I do. Drank it in here with him recently."

"Hey, Pilud Aches!" Lamar said, entering the café. "What's the good word?"

"The good word is *coffee*," Pilot X said, rounding on Lamar.

Lamar took a step back. "Whoa, brother. Is he drunk?" he said, looking at Glonda.

"I wish it were so," said Glonda. "But apparently they messed with dark forces and erased some bean drink he liked from history. Sounds like a net positive, if you ask me."

"Bean drink?" Lamar wrinkled up his nose. "Sounds awful."

"That's what I said," Glonda agreed.

Pilot X sunk down in his chair and took a bite of the stuffer. "Even the pie tastes different."

"Stop calling it that!" all three yelled at him at once.

Lamar took them to the bar and bought breek for Pilot X and Kayla. Glonda had to stay behind and work.

"So you made a machine that wiped out some rift thing that would have destroyed us all and somehow that also eliminated this drink called caffy made of beans," Lamar said.

"Yes, and we need to see what else it changed," Pilot X said.

"The fact that you don't know about the rift is not surprising," Kayla added. "The Institutes kept the danger of it from most Koheqi. So only interstellar pilots would have even cared about it, and then only as a navigational issue. What we did definitely saved Koheq. We're just trying to figure out the—"

"Side effects," Pilot X said.

"Well, what do you need to do that?" Lamar asked.

"I could quiz you on history," Kayla offered.

"You wouldn't learn anything except how much I suck at history," Lamar said.

"Well, then we need to look at records or something," Pilot X said, taking a sip of breek. He was starting to get used to the taste.

"I could borrow the news slider from the bartender. They let me look at it sometimes when I'm in here by myself." Lamar went to the bar and came back with a small screen. Kayla knew how to use it and began looking up historical info.

"The first Uniter is right. First flight looks right. First orbit is—probably right. I always confused this one, so either history changed to my wrong answer or I finally remembered it right. Founding of the Institutes looks right. The list of current Institutes looks right at a glance, though I admit I didn't have them all memorized," Kayla said.

"Verity, take a look," Pilot X said to his wrist device.

Her answer came to the device, so Pilot X read it to the other two. "She says it matches what she had. Oh, and she says to look up Henrina Canvill."

Kayla looked up the name. "Henrina Canvill. Minor trade freighter of the expansive period. That's when Koheq began to engage in trade with other stellar systems. Didn't do much, just ran some general goods and services with local group traders. Why?"

"Verity says Henrina Canvill was the first trader to bring coffee to Koheq."

"Oh," Lamar and Kayla both said at once.

"This is the entry Verity accessed previously. Here's what it used to say," Pilot X read from his wrist. "'Henrina Canvill led a trading group known as the Rift Riders. Their stated purpose was to use aggressive trade as a way to obtain scientific advancements to combat the complications to flight and navigation in the Koheqi system.'"

"That's because of the rift." Kayla nodded. "Keep reading."

Pilot X continued. "'Henrina Canvill went the farthest of all the Rift Riders and was the first to bring sotel, flacks, pineapples, hirsutian rope, and coffee to Koheq.'"

"I don't know what any of those things are. Except pineapple," Lamar said. "Everybody knows the Pineapple Planet. Best damned kids' stories ever!"

"I get it," Kayla mused. "Without the rift to motivate them, trade didn't push as far and didn't need to, once a good balanced amount came in. We've never been much of an aggressive trading society, preferring investigation. Canvill was an exception. Except without the rift to challenge her, her motivation was missing."

"And the coffee," Pilot X moaned.

Kayla and Pilot X left the bar together.

"Do you still have a house? . . . Do you have a house? I never saw you outside the Institute other than with Verity," he realized aloud.

"I have an apartment in the Institute. I spend almost no time there. I assume it's still there. I'm not looking forward to going back. I'm still processing all of this."

"You can stay in the singularity chamber tonight if you want. I can fix you up a guest room," Pilot X offered, hoping she'd say yes.

"I'd like that," she said.

"It's not really a guest room," Pilot X said, moving things around to make the room in the singularity chamber more comfortable, but constantly knocking things over or moving things he had just moved. "The ship isn't designed to carry passengers in the singularity. You really shouldn't use it during flight. But we're not flying, and you'd never know it was an old food-storage closet, would you?"

Kayla looked around. A lamp had been put on top of a stack of boxes marked *mushrooms*. The cot was partially shoved under a set of wire shelves that had been emptied of everything but a large can of something called *proles*. And the room generally smelled a bit like cheese.

"Never." Kayla made her best attempt at a smile.

"Well, good night," Pilot X said, and left before he ran out of things to say and do.

GOOD-BYE

ALEXANDRA STOOD WITH her back to Pilot X. Pilot X looked down and saw that he had flipped the switch on the Instant. But he could still see the lights of the ships in the sky.

"It's different, isn't it?" Alexandra said. "So many people saved this time. It's better."

"It's not," Pilot X said softly. "We had an effect. Things changed. Lives changed because of us. But at least this time it was not so devastating."

"That's what I mean. It's different."

Pilot X still felt the pain and guilt of what he had done, but it was smaller. Softer. Healing. It would never fully heal, but it was better. The confidence in himself that he had pretended to have now felt a little more real. Maybe this was the key. He wouldn't fix things so much as teach. He would use his experience to help others avoid the same mistakes. To make this universe—this new universe—better.

"It is different," Pilot X agreed. "Not perfect. But better."

"Better is a good goal," Alexandra said.

"That's what I'm going to do, Alexandra. I'm going to stop blaming myself. Stop blaming the Secretary. I'm going to start making things better. Maybe even in small ways. And certainly not always perfect. And I know I'll make mistakes. But I'll always be trying to make things better in everything I do. And then maybe I'll be able to forgive myself a little. I can't fix this. But I can make it better."

"What about me?" Alexandra asked.

He knew the answer. "I'm sorry, my love. I have to let you go. I'll always love you. But you're gone. I can't make you better. I can only remember how good you were."

"But I can be better," she said. And she turned. And there she was. Kayla. Not Alexandra.

Pilot X woke up with a smile.

TEAM

THE NEXT MORNING, they worked with Verity to identify any other anomalies, but found nothing significant or unexpected. The Rift Riders had still existed but called themselves the Rogue Riders because they broke with the norms of Koheqi society. But Canvill wasn't one of them and they didn't range as far. For the most part, the absence of the rift seemed to have left Koheqi society unaffected.

"Maybe keeping it a secret limited what things could change," Kayla suggested.

They went back into the retail ring so Pilot X could say a last good-bye to Glonda and Lamar. "If I ever get another pineapple, I'm bringing it to you," Pilot X said.

"Only because you want me to bake it into a stuffer." Glonda laughed. "Oh, wait right there." She popped into the back of the café and came back with a freeze-pack. It was a little powered block that kept anything in it frozen for several years.

"I saved you a pineapple stuffer. From my share. I knew you'd eat all yours. Keep this safe for a rainy day," she said. Then she hugged Pilot X, the hint of a tear in her eye. "I don't even know why I'm so emotional." She laughed again. "Or why I feel the need to thank you. But thank you."

It was the most touching change they'd witnessed. Glonda no longer knew why she would need to thank Pilot X. He wondered how reality solved for that. Verity had posited that a separate Pilot X and Kayla had been created in this reality who both traveled to where the rift would be and for some unknown reason just traded places. Kayla didn't like this idea, as it felt like cheating to her. Pilot X made Verity admit that her confidence in this being the correct explanation was "very small."

As Glonda turned to shake hands with Kayla, Lamar slapped Pilot X on the back and gave him a big hug of his own.

"I know why she's getting all emotional. You're a pretty decent guy there, Aches. And we don't see the likes of you often. We're going to miss you. Raise a glass of breek to me sometime, OK? May the sky bow to meet you."

Pilot X got tears in his eyes too. Lamar gave Kayla a big hug and then they headed back to Verity. Pilot X and Kayla hadn't spoken about her coming back to the landing lot to see him off. It just felt natural and they both let it happen without comment.

They walked up to the ship and Pilot X turned to say good-bye to Kayla. And there she was. Kayla. Not Alexandra. And he valued her the more for that change in him.

"Thank you, Kayla. You've helped me more than you can know. If you ever need anything. Ever. Just give a shout. Verity will let me know. Reluctantly, maybe." He shrugged. "But she will."

"Thank you for helping save my people, Pilot X. And for helping me do it right. I can never repay you for giving us our future back."

He didn't ask who she meant by *us*.

She laughed, brushing at her eye. "So. Where will you go now?"

"Where else? To discover the planet where coffee came from. You remember coffee. It has to bug you a little that it's gone."

"Yeah, I miss it too. And stuffers taste different now somehow."

"So it wasn't just me," Pilot X said. "See. Little things. Side effects."

"Also, I didn't make a big deal about it this morning, but my favorite grantball team's colors are now purple and gold instead of blue and white."

"Wanna come?" Pilot X said without thinking.

"I thought you'd never ask." She coughed a laugh that was part sob.

Pilot X took her hand and led her onto the ship. "Verity, get us prepared for takeoff. One passenger."

"I'm sorry, we do not have room for long-term passengers in flight in our current state of repair."

"You have access to an entire singularity, Verity," Pilot X said.

"That space is in use and restricted during flight."

"We won't be flying all the time. And she's coming with us, so you better just get used to it," Pilot X admonished her.

Verity paused. "I'll adjust the calculations, but we will need to set down for repairs at your hut."

"You have a hut?" Kayla asked.

"Oh, all the great time travelers have huts." Pilot X smirked.

"It's a very dirty place," Verity said.

"I don't mind getting my hands dirty," Kayla said. "I'll help with repairs."

"That will not be necessary," Verity said.

"People!" Pilot X said.

"I am not a person," Verity said.

"Oh, *now* she's not a person. Look, you two will figure this out. We have to fix the ship up and get flying. There's coffee to search for!"

"And people to help," Kayla added.

Pilot X just looked at her. He hadn't discussed his dream. "What do you mean?" he said. "All we have is the universe's only timeship and a nonlethal Trigor."

"I think she has had a good idea," Verity said.

"Now that's progress," Pilot X said. "I have a feeling things are going to keep getting better. Verity. Take us up!"

EPILOGUE

A KOHEQI COMMAND ship had observed the timeship
Verity when it returned to the landing lot in Syndrania after
escaping the pickle. As soon as it had landed and Kayla and
Pilot X had left to go meet Glonda and Lamar, the command
ship left orbit.

Koheqi ships were not meant for interstellar travel, but this
wasn't actually a Koheqi command ship and its occupants were
not Koheqi. They weren't even from that stellar system. They
had been observing Kayla for many orbits and were intrigued
and a bit alarmed at the progress she had made under Pilot
X. The woman on board had done some research and traced
Verity back through Vagson, Parthian Prime, and somehow all
the way to the planet with the hut.

They had been waiting for Pilot X to finally return to
Koheq and leave his ship before they felt safe making the trip.

Their ship dropped out of space and descended toward
the hut planet's surface, landing near the abandoned hut itself.
The man descended, followed by a woman in long, flowing red
robes that would look out of place in almost any society on any
planet or moon in the universe.

"It's in the hut," she said to him.

"Excellent. I'll get it at once."

He entered Pilot X's hut and rummaged around, coming out with nothing obvious in his hands. "Got it," he said.

"Let's stay here," the woman said. "But move somewhere less obvious."

"Other side of the planet?" he suggested.

"Just so," said the woman.

They landed their Koheqi command ship on the other side of the planet in an open clearing. They would have been visible from space if anyone was looking, but they weren't the kind to care. They had confidence that they'd never get caught and even if they did, they would figure their way out of it in a snap.

The man put out a table and two chairs and sat down in one. The woman sat down in the other. It was just the two of them on the whole planet for the moment. From inside his coat he pulled two folders. One was clearly marked *Trigor* and bore the stamps and markings of Institute research papers.

The other folder had no label.

"Shall we get to work, Asha?" the Secret Man asked. "The answer to this"—he tapped the unlabeled folder—"is somewhere in here." Then he tapped the Trigor folder and smiled.

GRAND PATRONS

Andrew Bradley
Bao Huy Duong
Bradd Schick
Chad Johnson
Chad S. Mawson
Christian Fletcher
Darrell A. Sullivan
Dave Laser
David Hayes
Jarrett Crowe
Jason Nicholson
Jason P. Peterson
Joseph M. Hager
Kevin Fournier
Kevin P. Robinson
Kyle Chapman
Marcus Kaczmarek
Matt 'doc' Brown
Michael J. Aikins

Mike McLaughlin
Nick Detweiler
Paul Dow
Paul M. Boyer
Peter Carrero
RockRollMartian
Richard David Turner, Sg
Ronald J. Richards
Scott Getman
Shana Martin
Sonia Vining
Stephen Young
Steven Judd
Susan Dannen
Raymond Thompson
Two Cows
Wayne Williamson

INKSHARES

INKSHARES is a reader-driven publisher and producer based in Oakland, California. Our books are selected not by a group of editors, but by readers worldwide.

While we've published books by established writers like *Big Fish* author Daniel Wallace and *Star Wars: Rogue One* scribe Gary Whitta, our aim remains surfacing and developing the new author voices of tomorrow.

Previously unknown Inkshares authors have received starred reviews and been featured in *The New York Times.* Their books are on the front tables of Barnes & Noble and hundreds of independents nationwide, and many have been licensed by publishers in other major markets. They are also being adapted by Oscar-winning screenwriters at the biggest studios and networks.

Interested in making your own story a reality? Visit Inkshares.com to start your own project or find other great books.